NOAH

HOUSE OF WILKSHIRE BOOK 2

KATHI S. BARTON

World Castle Publishing, LLC
Pensacola, Florida
Copyright © Kathi S. Barton 2018
Paperback ISBN: 9781949812435
eBook ISBN: 9781949812442
First Edition World Castle Publishing, LLC, December 10, 2018
http://www.worldcastlepublishing.com

Licensing Notes

Cover: Karen Fuller
Editor: Maxine Bringenberg

Chapter 1

Noah Farley stood as still as he could. Bringing attention to himself right now would get a great many people in trouble, especially him. Not that they wouldn't be anyway. Having him on site was just as bad to the police as having a taro reader, or even a magician, there with them when a crime needed to be solved. Not many believed in him. Nor did they believe he wasn't the person they were after nine times out of ten. But Noah got results, and that was important to a lot of people who did believe in him.

The man in charge of this investigation was someone that Noah not only didn't respect, but someone that he thought of as a lazy fuck. He thought that of a great many people, but this guy, Detective Peter Boseman, was the dictionary definition of the phrase—at least the word *lazy,* anyway. And the men that hung out with him—Noah called them his *crew*—were one step away from long prison terms or death by the state.

Either way, he'd be glad to be rid of them.

Boseman looked up at him. "I'm supposing you can see something that we can't? You look like you just know it all, and think that you're the best of the best, don't you? What is it, Farley? You seeing the ghosts of these here dead? What are they telling you about how they were killed?" Noah said nothing, again not moving. "Well, what I find here is this. The man murdered the woman, then killed himself. Over money. She was spending it—just look at them nails and shoes—and he wasn't having it. He's wearing old shoes that have been patched up and a dirty coat. Murder/suicide, end of case. Tell me, Farley, am I dead on?"

"No, not even close." He waited for someone, this man in front of him, to give him permission to speak again. He didn't need it. Just last week he'd been asked to become a part of the police force as a full-time consultant to the department. And he would have higher ranking than any man there, including Agent Boseman. But he'd not taken the job—wasn't even sure that he wanted it. He might take it just to put this man out to pasture.... No, he'd more than likely turn it down. He did this for the department because it gave him something to do. If it were a job, he knew he'd begin to hate it, and that wouldn't be good for anyone, especially the dead that needed justice— at least their families did. No, so long as he could come and go as he pleased, that was better for everyone—including Boseman again. He would be a dead detective if Noah had to work with him full-time.

"Not even close, am I now? Well, why don't you enlighten us about your powers of observation?" He snickered, and the men with him did the same. Noah thought that there was some sort of button that Boseman pushed to get reactions from the morons that were with him. "Go on. Tell me what you see that a thirty-year veteran of homicide can't see. And so's you know, I don't care what you see or observe, I know which one of us the captain is going to believe. And it ain't you."

"I'd not count on that if I were you. First of all, they didn't know each other to care enough about what kind of money either of them had. The man is someone that I've seen over on Welsher from time to time. I believe that he's homeless and pushes that cart that's right over there. You can see it—it has all his worldly goods in it. The woman is an office worker. The badge that is hanging from her purse there says that she works in finance. She had money to burn because she has no one else in her life. The reason I can see that is, there is no wedding band and her watch is worth more than you make in a year's time. The shoes are about four hundred, dress and coat another grand. I'd say she was a woman with good taste and liked to look nice. Her name is Shelby Kiddom, by the way. Again, it's on her name badge." The faerie that had been with him for decades, William, was in human form and recording the conversation for him for later use. Noah bent down to look at the things around the bodies. He spotted the police department issued gloves used at a crime scene, covered in blood, just under her left breast, and knew that only a cop would have those. Looking up, he knew who the killer was right away. The smirk gave him away.

"I'm assuming that some big shot guy like yourself would

know all about women's fashion and such. You wear it, Farley, when you're not wasting the taxpayers' money? Or do you have a personal knowledge with this man? You know...?" Boseman did the international sign, one Noah had seen used a million times, for fucking. "Are you a homo, Farley?"

Ignoring his crude comments, Noah continued. "The male, I would say in his mid to late sixties, came upon the woman to offer aid. She was already dead by then, and the man that had killed her, not a husband, was just waiting for a flow of traffic of people so he could blend in. There is no blood splatter on this man, and there would be if he'd been the one to cut her throat. The male just happened upon him as Shelby was bleeding out. She had her throat slit from behind, but the killer would have had blood all over him. The homeless man has a single gunshot to the head — from behind as well."

"And you got all that from looking at two dead bodies? I won't believe it. Nobody will." He looked around at his crew, the only thing that Noah would call the cops with him. "He must be one of them there clara-boinks. You know, the ones that can see the dead?"

The button must have been pushed again, because they all laughed like they had before. Short and loud. One of them even sounded like a jackass braying. All in a day's work for Noah, he thought, putting up with idiots. Stretching his neck as he stood up, he smiled at Boseman.

"It's clairvoyant, and that's not primarily what I am. I'm a profiler, for lack of a better term." Boseman laughed harder. "Yes, well, if you ever get off your fat fucking ass and look into this, you'll find that the man who killed them both is standing with you right now. It's a cop."

Noah and William walked away. When he heard the shots being fired, he didn't turn back, but did pull out his cell phone. Telling dispatch that there was an officer down and giving them the address, he kept walking to his car. William, a faerie, changed into his other self and landed on his shoulder.

"We can only hope that the man killed Boseman too." William said that he'd not. "Figures. I need to get away for a while. I know that I was only just asked to take a full-time position at the station, but I can't do this right now. I need time to grieve. I know that my family has been gone for some time, but I still ache from their passing. I understand why they did it, but my heart still hurts from it."

"As I have said to you many times, your lordship." William was the only person who knew that not only was Noah a dragon and someone who could solve a crime quickly, but he was also—he *had* also been—the king of a castle. "If you remember, sir, his lordship Devon invited you to his home for the summer months. He has taken a wife, and she is breeding his child now."

"Yes, I remember." As they got into the car, William sitting on his own perch on the next seat, Noah continued. "I hate this city. Well, not the city so much as the people here. And I think they get more violent and more stupid with each passing year. I just need to get away from this. I need to be with friends who care not what I can do or what I am."

"The city and the people it consists of are the same thing, as I have pointed out to you before." Noah nodded and laughed. "You do need a vacation, if you don't mind me saying so. But you also need to be your dragon for longer periods than a few minutes when the rain is coming down. Sir, he needs to be himself as badly as, if not more than, you."

He thought about the vacation for the rest of the drive to his home. He was going to do it, but the amount of work that he had to do and to delegate before leaving was going to be a great deal. But still, he thought that everyone would enjoy it, getting away for a time.

Noah pulled into the driveway and looked at the home that he shared with about fifty other beings. The house looked like one of the hundreds of other houses in the city and was a cookie cutter of the ones on his street. At least on the outside. Once you were inside, that was where you really saw the difference. It was about ten times larger than the other houses and filled with things that he'd collected over the years. Magic and the beings that lived with him, all faeries, had given him that and more. Companionship for the most part, and that he treasured more than anything else.

There were three floors to the home, but it only showed that there was one from the outside. The kitchen was big enough for several of the finest chefs to make a meal and never touch one another. A dining room that was wasted on him could easily feed over a hundred guests. Even his bedroom— about twice the size of the entire house next to his, which was a couple of acres away—was something that his magic had done for them when he and William took up residence. The others, faeries that had been at his castle home, had come to live with him when he lost it due to taxes not being paid on time.

When he'd purchased the home, there had been nothing around the area but fields of tobacco and corn. Then as the houses started to pop up, so did the fence that he had around his property. And now it was electrified too. He knew that people thought him to be something of a recluse, which he supposed he was. Noah preferred his own company over anyone else's, save William.

His staff, the faeries, were there waiting for him as soon as he entered. "There is a call from a Lady Wakefield. She said that she is the marchioness to the House of Wilkshire." He paused in going up the staircase when Rose cleared her throat. "She giggled, sir. Giggled and said that I was just to call her Kelly, not the mouthful that is her title from being married to Lord Devon. I don't understand."

He turned to look at his staff and realized that they were just as curious. He thought about what he'd heard about Kelly, as Lady Susanna had called her, and knew that she was just as delightful as she'd told him. Noah sat down on the stairs and laughed.

"I've been thinking that we'd all go for a visit to the Marquess Devon and his new family. Please, I would like for you all to close up the house. Donate all the foodstuff to the shelter, and pack us whatever we might need to travel to England." He looked at William as he continued. "I want you to gather up the seeds and other things that you've been hoarding, and we'll take them someplace where they can thrive. We will all leave as soon as arrangements can be made."

"Sir, what about your job?" He didn't care and told

William that. Noah didn't need the money, not really, and he had to get away. "Shall I tell them that there has been an emergency and that you must travel today?"

"Yes, that would be splendid. Also, do me a favor and find me Devon's number." Rose handed him the small sheet of paper with not only the phone number, but also how many times Kelly had called. "It seems, my dear family, that we're headed home. I only hope that we'll receive a better welcome than we have before."

The cheer went up and Noah stood up. He never said this, not anymore, but he wondered if things could get any worse. They could and would, he knew, but for now, he'd take it as it came.

By nightfall he'd gotten a call from his boss at the station. Noah had told him everything that he'd told Boseman, and that the man in his little posse was the murderer. Noah told him that Boseman had been an ass. Also, he wasn't one hundred percent sure, but he thought that Boseman had known about it.

"Yes, well, that's the way he operates. Or I should say, the way that he did. I was hoping that with you in charge of him, he'd either quit or he'd have to be fired. I got the recording of the events, and I'm going to ask him, quite firmly, to retire before I have to fire him. I have three men dead because of his stupidity, as well as two more injured. And all because he wouldn't listen to you when you spoke to him last week. This couple, the ones that were killed needlessly, they're going to be added to that list. And Roberts, the murderer, he's dead. You didn't ask, but I wanted you to know that Roberts been taken off the streets." Noah had told Boseman, as well as Detective Captain Lin Ming, that there were two dirty cops on the force. Boseman told him he was wrong, Captain Ming told him to look into it. "I'll talk to you when you return. If there is anything you need, just let me know, Noah. I don't want to lose a good man like you."

By mid-morning the next day, not only were they on their way, but he'd been able to bring everyone on his staff, all faeries, on his body. It was something else that he'd been given, the ability to bring with him and use as many faeries as he could put upon his body. They not only were able to travel with him without anyone seeing them, but they lent him a great deal of power, power that was much different than that of his parents.

Noah smiled when he thought of when he'd called Devon. "I'm so glad that you're coming. Grandmother will be back by the time you arrive, if not at the same time." He looked over at the marchioness, who had hitched a ride with him on his plane—the last of his inheritance from the castle. "Also, we have been making some improvements here. Some that I'm betting that you will be pleased with. We're going to be working very hard here to make sure that you never leave us again."

It wouldn't take much, not with the way he was feeling. It all depended on the welcome he received when he arrived. Would they greet him with open arms, or would they simply turn their backs on him as they had done before? Not Devon, but the town in general.

"How is that lovely wife or yours, Devon? She must be

sick of you by now. Perhaps I can persuade her to come back with me, and we'll have a bunch of little dragons." He was only joking, and he knew that Devon knew it. "I talked to your grandmother while she was visiting my area. She is quite taken with the little slip of a woman."

"She has my mom's dragon, Noah. Had I not been standing there when it happened, I think I would never have believed it. And, I think that we're all in a better place too. Knowing that my mom was killed by my father gave us some peace that I didn't think I'd have after he was dead. It gave me some closure that I didn't have before." He knew that from talking to his plane mate. It had given Lady Susanna closure as well. "When you arrive, I'll have someone meet you at the airport. I'm having one put in for us here, now that I have a wife, so that it will be much easier for us to travel without the world knowing."

Noah knew what he meant—so that someone wouldn't be able to take Kelly. It had happened before. Someone had gotten it in their head to take one of Devon's stepmothers. That had ended badly when Devon's father had refused to pay the ransom, saying that she was unfit as a wife to a marquess anyway. They had taken their anger out on the young woman, and she'd suffered brutally from the beating and the resulting wounds.

"I should be there in a couple of days. These days the only thing that I have left is the plane, and that will be gone soon too. Also, I have a great many faeries with me, and they'd like to see if they can work with yours. I have also had William gather some of his seeds from the homestead that you can plant there. If you don't mind." He told him that was fine, and that they'd been looking at places for him to stay when he decided to stay for good. "You and that little wife of yours, you're plotting? My goodness, Devon, you surely have become a changed man. I think I might stay, for a time anyway. As for homes, I'm not sure about that right now. I'm a little short on funds that I can readily put my hands on at the moment, as you well know."

"I do. And I understand. Whatever you want to do, my home is always open to you." And he knew that as well. For as many times as people had said that to him over the decades, Noah knew that Devon meant it. "Once you get here, you will never want to leave again. I am so positive about it that I'm going to throw a dinner party to welcome you. I've missed you, Noah. I'm so glad that you're finally coming for a visit."

"I've missed you as well, my friend. I'll see you soon."

As they flew to their destination, Noah and Susanna talked about the new Devon. Yes, he thought to himself, this was going to be a very good visit. And who knew, perhaps he'd end up staying, as Devon wanted.

~*~

Laura watched her daughter struggle with her temper. The fact that she was trying to hold onto it said that she was trying to change, and not just go from zero to overboard when people made her pissy. However, if Laura had been talking to the man, she would have murdered him by now. The man was as dense as a cinderblock.

He'd come to the front door about twenty minutes ago, screaming and accusing almost as soon as the door opened an

15

inch. And when he'd been told that the police were going to be called, he yelled louder, making sure, Laura thought, that the world knew he was upset. She listened to Bryce as she tried in vain to convince the man she didn't have his daughter.

"I said, six times now, that I can't help you find your daughter. If she told you that she was coming here, then you can bet that I'd tell you if she was. Emma and I are not friendly enough to be going to one another's homes." He asked why not. "Because I don't like her. Not one bit. And you can bank on that too. If she was hoping I'd cover for her, then she's just as shit out of luck as you are."

"I have it written down right here on this note she left for me two days ago. I want you to read it." Bryce snatched it from Emma's father and read the note as one might to a child. "You are a nasty, rude person."

"Precisely. Now, call the police, call the national guard. They'll have better luck finding her than you will here at my home." Bryce started to close the door in Mr. Sharp's face. He put his foot in the way so that Bryce couldn't close it. "Look. I've tried very hard, several times, not to punch you in the face. But if you don't remove your foot from the doorway, I'm going to pull out a knife and cut the part off that is preventing me from closing my door and close it. I'm tired and out of sorts, and you're not helping one bit."

He jerked his foot back and Bryce slammed the door. As she leaned her back against it, Mr. Sharp started pounding on the door's other side. The man had a death wish, that was all Laura could think about him.

"Do you know where she is?" Bryce nodded and walked

away from the door into the kitchen. Laura followed her. Her mother-in-law, Bea, was sitting at the table, a cup of tea stirring in front of her. "Bea, I thought that as long as there was the possibility of someone seeing you, you'd not use your magic in this house."

"Yes. But he wasn't going to get in. We both know that. Bryce would have cut him to ribbons. Or if he got this far, I would have changed him into a toad. Nasty man that." Bea picked up her cup of tea and the spoon disappeared. "You know where she is, Bryce, honey?"

"Dead." No one said anything. If Bryce said she was dead, then she was dead. "I was wondering if we could have chicken and dumplings for dinner. We could use the roasted chicken from last night, since we'd be getting a late start."

Laura looked at Bea, who simply shook her head. Sometimes she was jealous of the two of them, the things that they could share. But on this, Laura was glad for the fact that she wasn't anymore a witch than the dog was next door. Her daughter was very powerful, and her mother-in-law was a close second.

They talked about dinner for a little while more, none of them very hungry, it seemed. As they plotted and planned for tomorrow, Bryce ate some grapes, a bowl of them on the table that hadn't been there before. Tomorrow Bryce was going into the police station to turn down the job that they'd asked her to take.

"I can't be working around people all the time and not have one of them notice that I'm off my noddle." Bea smacked Bryce's hand. "Well, I don't think that, but you know that

17

they will once I use my magic. And I will. Even if I only have to turn one of them into something that is silent."

"I don't blame you there. While our kind isn't burned at the stake anymore, I do think that they'd put you away and never find the key if they knew just how powerful you are. Not that a cell would hold you, but then they'd try something else. Oh, by the way, that man next door thinks that his doggy is dead. I've taken care that his little doggy is safe. Poor thing. He was hurting it again and letting it stand in the snow all night." Laura asked Bea where he was. "Under the table, now that you're aware of him. He's a good dog. I might train him to be my animal. I've been sort of lonely without Pet around."

It was a startling revelation that witches had familiars. It was even more surprising that they didn't necessarily have to be a cat—any animal would do. Case in point, Bryce had a bird. It was a pretty cockatoo that spoke four languages and could curse better than a sailor on leave. His name was Fred.

Pet, Bea's animal, had died. He'd been a pretty little lizard that would chase Laura around the kitchen when he was being playful. It could do more than snap out his tongue at her when she spoke to him, as he too was as powerful as his mistress.

They were sure that he'd been poisoned by someone, but who had done it was a mystery. She thought it was a neighbor, but she didn't ask anymore what they'd do to him if it had been him. Some things were better left unknown, Laura had figured out.

Few knew that they were a house of witches. Laura could do some magic, gifted to her by Bea first, then Bryce had given her more. Laura couldn't do spells, nor could she cast, gathering ingredients like she would for a cake and putting them together for some use. Laura could help with spells, but she wasn't able to cast them on someone or something. That was fine by her as well.

"I was thinking about that trip. The one where we headed back to your old country." Laura got up and started throwing together a salad. That was something that she knew would be eaten, even if it wasn't right now. She wouldn't be going on the trip—that was something that Bea and Bryce did twice a year. "I've heard about some herbs that we can gather and bring back with us. It would be nice to have a fully functioning garden."

"It would at that. I have that castle too. The one that was up on the market for non-payment of taxes. We could all stay there."

Laura wanted to see the castle in person—it was supposed to be grand. But she'd stay here, hold down the fort, so to speak, and they'd bring her back all manner of things as gifts.

Laura tuned them out. There was nothing she could have added to the conversation other than to find out when they were leaving and when they'd return. As she was putting the bowl filled with the best greens she could find in the fridge, Bryce asked her if she was paying attention.

"I was. You two will be leaving and I'll make sure that the animals are safe here. I'll need to have someone help me with the mail. I can't travel all that far without having my hip hurt me a great deal." She'd fallen two years ago, and her hip hadn't been the same since. And the doctors told her that it

19

wasn't broken, just badly bruised. Quacks. "I know you won't have to pack anything, so tell me what you need for me to do."

"Pack for yourself." Laura started shaking her head. "Yes, you're going with us this time. No excuses. I told you the last time you were going with us the next time. So, you pack you what you think you might want to take, and I'll close up the house. Grandma said she'd take care of everything else. This will be an adventure for all of us, I think."

"Bryce, I'm too much trouble." Her daughter crossed her arms over her chest and tapped her foot. "You are not using my way of getting you to mind me. You just go with Bea and I'll be here when you return. I'm too hurt to want to sit on a plane for hours."

"We're not. Returning, I mean." She asked her what she meant. "Grandma said that it's time that we move on. People are beginning to notice that she's not aging. Neither am I. And you look like we could be sisters and not mother and daughter. It's time, Mom. We've done it before, and we need to do it again. And even if we weren't, you're still going."

The hand on her shoulder buzzed like electric through a cord all the way through her body. Laura stood there for several seconds, the warm feeling of good health still making her slightly light headed. She knew that when she moved around, she'd be not only as good as new, but also not in any more pain.

Sitting in the chair that was still warm from when Bea had been sitting in it, she looked at Bryce. "I told you not to ever do that. I'll not have you wasting your talents on an old woman like me. I do feel better, but you shouldn't have done that. Honey, I knew that you'd have to move on soon. I just thought that you'd just make me old and leave me behind. I mean, that's what I'd do."

"You would not. If you don't pack, I will, and you know that I'll accidently leave something behind. You can't think that I'd leave you here, do you?" She shook her head. "Good. Pack only what you can't replace. Then when we get to this castle, we'll buy what you need. And if you pack up a box of things too big for your suitcase, tell me and I'll send it along too."

"What about Emma's body? You have to give that man some closure. Not that he deserves it, but you should at least let someone find her." Bryce said that she couldn't and got up from the table.

Laura sat there for several more minutes. Bryce couldn't help the ones that had killed themselves. It was a vow that she'd taken when she'd taken her first lesson at the school for witchcraft. Everyone had to give up something, some kind of thing, that they couldn't help humans with, and she'd said that she'd never help the suicide victims' bodies to be found. It was something that she didn't run into often, but this time she knew that it hurt her little girl. It was the only thing that Bryce could think of to give up that wouldn't be her. Those were the only choices that she'd been given—give up her mother or the victims of suicide.

Getting up, Laura started a mental list of things that she was going to take. Most of it was pictures, but there were a few things that she had been given by her late husband. Austin had been a good man, but he was also one that didn't hide his magic. It was what had gotten him killed by the witch council.

Chapter 2

Bryce loved the old worldliness of the castle. The town, too, was something right out of a storybook in the way it looked and how the people acted. She had been welcomed, her entire family, and she was glad for that. If they were curious as to what they were, and she was sure they were interested, they were never rude enough to inquire. Bryce also heard that there was a dragon couple nearby. She would avoid them as much as she could.

It's not that they couldn't get along. Dragons and witches hadn't been mortal enemies for a long time. It was said that a witch was the one that had made the first dragon, to get back at a spurned lover. But Bryce no more believe that than she did most stories that she'd heard.

Bryce didn't care for the large shifters. They were usually clumsy, overbearing know it alls. Laughing to herself as she made her way around their new home, she stopped when she saw the man walking along the garden just beyond where she was. Her grandmother greeted him as she usually did a stranger, with a hug and a kiss on his cheeks. If he was startled by it or thought her odd, he didn't look to show it. Knowing that her grandmother would be safe no matter what the man did to her, she flew to the top of the castle and sat on one of the many turrets that looked out over the smallish town.

It had all the elements of a good place to live. A grocery store that had a great many items that were locally made. A hardware store that also doubled as a post office when needed. And there was even a shoe repair place. She saw a few other buildings, but from her vantage point, she couldn't make out what they might be. As she was thinking of going into the town, just to have a look around, a small thud behind her had her turning. The dragon turned to man in a heartbeat.

"Don't jump. Life can't be all that bad." She just turned her back to him, hoping that he'd get the message. "I'm Noah. You must be Bryce."

"Why are you here?" He didn't answer her this time. "I'm sure that you know that you're trespassing. Just go away and I'll pretend that I didn't see you."

"Ah, but you did, and we both know it. Are you planning to jump? I have to tell you, this isn't just a little jump. You'd really harm yourself if I were to allow you to fall that far." She looked at him. "I'm charming like that."

"You're neither charming nor going to save me. Had I wanted to jump, I'd have not waited until someone would come to rescue me. I've been about as polite as I can be today. Go away." He laughed, and she felt a returning smile tug at her mouth. "You're very rude."

"No, you're the one that is being rude. So far I've tried to introduce myself, given you a part of myself in showing you that I was a dragon, and tried to save you. You've been nasty and rude and didn't tell me that you were all right." She looked out over the town again. "You and your family, you've purchased my home. I mean, you got it fair and square, but I grew up here behind these keep walls, and would be willing to give you a tour of the things you might not have gotten from the brochure."

"We're not human either, so if there were hidden places, I'm sure that my grandmother has found them. And I wasn't being rude so much as I was trying very hard to let you know that I don't care for company. Not just yours, but any company. As for jumping?" She leapt off the building and hovered there for several seconds before drifting down to the ground.

Bryce made her way to the front of the castle. She heard the man's laughter and it made her smile again. Twice in one day. She had no idea what it was about this man that made her want to bash his head in one moment and make him laugh the next. Bryce had a feeling that, like her, he didn't do that very much.

Her mom was in the kitchen familiarizing herself with the pantry as well as the big stove. It was large too, and now she knew why. To feed a family of dragons, the stove as well as all the cooking items in this room would have to be large to accommodate the amount of food one of them would eat. Not to mention a family of them.

"I've met one of the previous owners of the castle. They were dragons." Her mom looked at her; there were three pencils tucked in her hair at various places. She was making a list, it seemed. "He said that there are places to hide in here. I'm guessing that Grandma found them already."

"She said that she knew of a few places that she'd show me. Are we worried about the townspeople?" Bryce took one of the pencils out of her mom's hair when she seemed to be looking for one. "Thanks. I'm having a hard time focusing today."

"It's the time change, and the fact that this place is covered in magic. I've not taken the time to see who put it here, but it's strong. When are you going into town?" She said in about an hour. "I'd like to go with you if you don't mind. And in answer to your question, no, I don't think we have anything to worry about here. In fact, I'd guess that with dragons here, they're used to having people be ageless."

Nodding, her mom told her that she'd let her know when they were leaving. Making her way up the long winding staircase from the kitchen to the upper floors, she thought about the man. A dragon, of all things. And he was close enough to the house to pop over whenever he wanted to.

Her room was in one of the turrets, the narrowest one. Her bed, a large one that had been left behind by the dragon family, was sitting facing the window rather than the headboard covering it. She loved waking up to the sun coming into her room and had decided that she'd never put curtains up.

The castle was modern, with indoor plumping and large

walk-in closets. There was also Internet and cable throughout the house. Not that they owned a television, but it was nice to be able to hook up to the Internet. She sat down at her laptop and let the Witches' Council know where she was, as well as how long she'd be staying.

Bryce didn't need to let them know, but she did it because she wasn't going to break rules that might change at the drop of a hat. Her grandmother had told her that the council would change the rules and laws to suit themselves. That was what had gotten her father killed.

He'd been teaching her some of the finer points to casting magic, and he'd been doing it in their backyard. But someone — the neighbor, who had also been a witch — told on him. And as she rarely let anything go when the council said that they'd take care of it, they'd banished him, then had one of their dragons — there were a great many of them back in the day — kill him when she wasn't satisfied.

It wasn't why she didn't care for dragons. The dragon had only been doing what he'd been told to do. And after a few weeks, gems had shown up on their doorstep. The note with them had told how he'd loved her father and found him to be a good and kind man. And he wanted her to have a part of his tears so that she could continue her education as a great witch.

Bryce had done that, and more. Every time she met a new witch, older or younger, Bryce spent as much time with them as they'd allow, learning as much as they'd let her, taking their spells and adding them to her own book. Her grandmother had given hers to Bryce when she'd been just a fledgling.

Now that she'd claimed it as her own, the book had doubled in thickness, and the pages were now all her own.

The trip to town with her mom was nice. They couldn't walk—it was much too far—but while there they found two shops going in, as well as a building that was devoted to just local items. As soon as she entered, Bryce paused at the doorway and looked around.

"Bryce?" She shook her head at her mom and told her to wait with her. As they stood there, Bryce dug deeper into the room, letting her magic flow over it to find what had disturbed her. Just as she found it, a woman came toward her and put out her hand. As her mom was reaching for it, Bryce smacked it down.

"We don't want any trouble." The woman nodded but didn't smile or put her hand down. "We've only just moved here, and we want no trouble with you or your kind."

"You've already caused me trouble, witch. And I aim to make sure that you don't do anything more." When she raised her hand up, Bryce did the same. Almost as soon as she shoved magic at the woman, she felt her mom move, disappearing from behind her.

With no time to look, she held her magic and watched the woman in front of her. Bryce knew the exact moment that the other woman realized that she was in over her head. Backing away from her, the woman seemed to know it was much too late for that. Bryce didn't destroy her, as she was supposed to do, but spoke calmly as she held her in her place.

"You started this. And I am well within my rights to take you." She nodded. Her name was March—no last name was hers to have, but she went by something entirely different. "March the faerie of the disenchanted, I give you one chance to redeem yourself."

"Nay. You should be bowing before me, queen of the witches. We both know that I have an army at my beck and call." Reaching beyond where they stood, Bryce found the faerie queen and begged her forgiveness, but said she needed her help. As soon as she appeared before March, the banished faerie fell to the floor. "You come to her aid, but when I needed you, you ignored my pleas for help?"

"I come to her because she has not tried to have me murdered in my gardens. Bryce, a Frost witch of great standing and good morals, hasn't tried to kill millions of my kind in the name of making herself queen. No, I did not come to your aid because it was a trap—a trap to not only kill your queen, but to kill many of your own kind." The faerie was changed into her true self. "What did you hope to gain by taking on a witch? This witch in particular? I'm assuming that she asked you to stand down, that she gave you a chance to live another day?"

"You wish to kill me?" That was the only thing that the faerie got out of what she had been asked. Not answering the questions so that she might well live another day but knowing that the queen was actually thinking of ending her life. "You cannot. I will not allow you to take out one such as myself."

"Noah, come forth." The man from the castle was suddenly in the room, and with him were Bryce's mom and another man. "This faerie has caused you much trouble. She has threatened what is yours that you've yet to claim. She and her kind have destroyed fields of food for the others. Poisoned waterways in the name of justice—a justice that I do not understand. You have all rights, Noah Farley, Earl of Dragons Keep, Lord to the Sheppard lands, to do with her as you would see fit."

Bryce was confused. The man was an earl, as well as a lord. Why was he hanging around a castle, that by all rights belonged to him, and not claiming it? Then there was the fact that the queen had said that he'd yet to claim something. When it occurred to her what she might be talking about, her magic holding March slipped.

~*~

Noah didn't laugh. He wanted to, badly, but he was slightly afraid that if he did it again, she'd do as she'd threatened and knock his head off. Not that she could, but he wasn't willing to take any chances with Bryce. As Donald, Devon's physician, stitched up the wound on her shoulder, Noah thought of what she had said to him after the faerie had been destroyed.

"I will not be a mate to you." Noah had wisely said nothing. At least he had thought it was wise. "Did you hear me? Or did you hit your head harder than I had hoped?"

"You wish me harm? Nay, I don't believe that. But no, I didn't hurt my head. I'm simply trying to judge how angry you are so that you don't hurt me. Again." She growled at him and then cried out in pain. "You might think that you're very bad assed when you do that, but I simply find you adorable. Does your mother know how cute you are when you're upset? Oh, by the way, she's lying down upstairs. I

30

think all this must have— I cannot believe how adorable you are."

"Noah, I don't think you're helping." He looked over at Devon, who was also having a hard time keeping a straight face. "She's saved us a great deal of grief today, and I think perhaps we should be grateful rather than pissing her off."

"My goodness." He looked up, being pulled from his thoughts when Grandma Susanna spoke. "I know who you are, don't I? My goodness child, but you have grown into a great beauty. How are your father and mother?"

"My father is dead." No one said anything, but the elderly Frost woman hit Bryce on the shoulder. "Well he is, isn't he?"

"Yes, he is, but I think you could say that a good deal nicer. After all, that young man there saved your mother's life." Bea huffed before continuing. "And when I asked him why he'd not taken over and kept you safe, do you know what he said? That you had it covered. Well, that should get him points in the right direction."

"Why don't you all go away and let me rest?" This time Noah did laugh. "And what the fuck do you find so funny? And I swear to you, Grandma, you hit me again and I'll go back to the States and hide from you all."

"Like you could do that. You're my flesh and blood, child." Bea stood up and so did he. "You're a good man, Noah. And I'm sorry to tell you this, but you are going to have your hands full with this one. By the way, your parents—I was very sorry to hear about their demise. That shouldn't have happened to such good people."

"Thank you." He hugged her. When everyone had left

the room but Bryce, himself, and Donald, he waited while he finished bandaging her up and left before he spoke again. "I'm assuming that you understand that we're mated."

"No—what I understand is that you think we're mated. I have no desire to be mated. Not at the moment, nor anytime in the future. I have enough going on right now with every fucking witch in the world coming to try and knock me off so they can have my power."

"I got a part of it too." She looked at him, and even though she looked to understand what he meant, Noah explained. "I got a portion of the faerie's magic when you did. I wasn't sure that there was any to be had, but I got a bit of it."

"I didn't want you to kill her. Not just you, but anyone. I doubt that she'd have changed her ways, but I always hope they will." Noah nodded as Bryce struggled to stand up. He stood to help her, but she waved him off. "This is your home. Why was my grandma able to get it, and why did it go so cheaply?"

"My parents were fucked over, much like your father was. Not by the council, but someone just as much a pain in the ass. They were living their life like they had for hundreds of years, taking in stray dragons that needed a place to stay for one reason or the other, and giving enough of themselves to heal the community, as well as the town itself. One day a larger dragon came through the town, decided that he loved the home as much as we did, and decided to take it. And to do that, he killed my father. My mom died of a broken heart. But in the end, he didn't get the castle either."

"You killed him." He told her that Devon had. "I see.

And Devon, he's something more than your run-of-the-mill dragon."

"Yes, he's a marquess." She asked how that made a difference. "Like you being powerful because of your magic, because of his title and his magic — not to mention money — he was able to take on the man and end his life. Sadly, however, he couldn't own the castle that was deemed a dragons' keep, and I could no longer own it because my father, rightly so, lost it when our accountant said he was paying the taxes on it and decided to take off with the money instead."

"That's the stupidest thing I've ever heard." Noah shrugged and told her that he was sure she had just as many stupid rules of her kind. "Yes, well, you have a point there. I am sorry to hear about them. My father lost his life to a busybody. The council did it — the Witches' Council — but he lost it all the same. A dragon ended his life."

"I heard." He would have heard much more if he'd not been grieving for the loss of his parents at the time. "Your mother — she's not a witch, is she?"

"No. She married my father as a human. Mom is much more than that now, thanks mostly to what Grandma and I have given her." She moved out of the room she was in, which also happened to have been his bedroom when he lived here. "I don't want you hanging around here. You and I — while it sounds great to have you as a mate, I just don't want you around to have to pick up the pieces after something happens to me."

"Nothing will." She was three steps down when she stopped to turn to him. "I didn't do anything to change you, but you're not going to be harmed by any witches that come for you. Didn't you hear what Dawn said about you? You're the queen of witches."

"I've heard that before." She continued down the stairs, talking to him as she went. Noah followed, having no choice in the matter. And he found that he didn't care. Wherever she went, he was going too. In the kitchen, Noah asked her why she didn't believe it. "Today, when that faerie was ready to remove my head, I had to call on help to take care of her. Not just for my mom—and thank you for that—but with the faerie herself. I couldn't have done it on my own."

"Yes, you could have. And I think you know that. However, it doesn't make you a weak witch to have to call for help. It makes you a smart one. Also, someone that doesn't get in over her head about magic." She snorted at him and opened the brand-new refrigerator. Blue plastic was still covering a great deal of it. "That should be empty, right? Why have one at all if you can fill it at whim?"

"It's not for us, it's for nosey people—you, in case you're wondering. What do you want to eat? I can make you just about anything. I'm having a roast beef sandwich on rye." He told her that he'd have the same. "I don't do chips or stuff like that. If, however, you think of something you'd like to have with your meal, it'll be in the cabinet above the fridge."

He really didn't want anything except the sandwich and to be able to sit with her a while and talk. But thinking of something that he'd not had in ages, he wasn't the least bit surprised to find it in the cabinet just where she'd said it would be. Pulling down the onion flavored rings, he sat down at the table and asked for some tea.

Noah ate about half of his food before he spoke again. He wanted to know all about her and her family but started telling her about his own. When his glass was empty, he started to stand to refill both their glasses when she touched her finger to his. As the glass filled, Noah laughed again.

"You find a great many things humorous, don't you? I mean, you laugh at the strangest things. Up on the roof, I had a feeling that you didn't do that much—laugh, I mean. But now you seem to do it all the time." Noah told her that he'd not had a very good life up until now. "Yeah, me either. I love my mom and grandma. They've been there for me when I've fallen on my face. But it's also been difficult where we lived before. Changing ourselves to meet their expectations was difficult, to say the least—our not growing old. I have a feeling that it's not going to matter all that much to the people around here, is it?"

"No, so long as you don't hurt them in any way—not with their livelihoods nor their own lives. They pretty much keep to themselves. Devon, he lives nearby, but not within this community. He is a good man, better than his father ever was. Now he was a horrific man."

"Grandma told me what she'd been able to find out about the dragons around here." Noah asked her why she didn't care for dragons. "I think, and you are a prime example of this, they're overbearing. I guess that's wrong too. I don't know. It has nothing to do with the death of my father, if that's what you're thinking. I just have never had a fondness for them."

"And me? Me being a dragon, is that going to be an issue

35

for you?" Bryce asked him why, was he going to change himself? "No, that's not what I meant. If you're afraid of me, then I'll tread carefully when I shift. If you hate my kind, I'll do the same. But if it's something that I can change your mind about, then I'd like to be able to do that. If you'll allow it."

Bryce stood up, gathering the plates as she did. Instead of washing them or even loading them into the new dishwasher that was there, she simply put then on the counter and they put themselves away, clean and dried.

"Dragons have a great many parts to them that a witch like me could use for casting and such. What do you think would happen if someone came gunning for me, and found out that a very old and powerful dragon was her mate?" He nodded, understanding more than he could explain to her at the moment. "So, this other witch, or warlock, they come here knowing that if they kill me, or my grandmother — who is a great witch herself — then they'd get more than they bargained for; or for that matter, could have thought of getting. What I mean is, they'd have the means to make some very powerful and very deadly magic, because they'd have us both."

"No, they'd never get past me to get to either you or your grandmother." Bryce told him he was missing the point. "I don't think so. I might give you the impression that I'm sort of laid back. But having you as my mate, that's a game changer for me. Basically, you'd be my priority, over myself."

"I don't want that." Noah told her it was much too late for that. "If you get hurt, for any reason, I'd never forgive myself."

"Because you feel responsible for your father's death."

He watched her struggle with what he'd said. He'd known, even before speaking to Laura, that Bryce blamed herself for her dad's death. "You couldn't have known that the neighbor next to you wasn't complaining at all. It was all made up. Black is a liar and a cheat. Killing your father was no more something that needed to be done than him asking for you to leave your mother behind. The other two should have known that. That's why there is always an alternate to fill the space."

"But Father's dead. Because I wanted to be the best there was." He asked her if she was. "Yes. I'm the strongest witch there is."

Chapter 3

The gardens were coming along. Bea had started out slowly on them, not wanting to draw too much attention to the fact that she was helping them along. But when Noah had shown up with his faerie William, she had made it just what she wanted, even planting most of the herb seeds that she'd been gifted in the much larger garden.

"You need a tractor." Smiling, she looked at Laura. "I didn't think it was this big when you started back here. But I can see now that you have not just a larger garden, but a drying house as well."

"I do, thanks in part to Noah. Did you know that this was his home at one time? He told me that this garden was a favorite of his mothers. And up the hill there is another one, filled with the wild things that she couldn't bring down here." Laura sat on the bench that Bea had put in just that morning. "What brings you away from your new kitchen?

I'm assuming that it has something to do with the dragon or your daughter."

"Both, actually. She's trying her best to keep him at arm's length. I don't think it's going to work. He's going to charm his way to her." Bea didn't think that would work very well either, but let Laura continue. "I've invited him to live in the castle with us. I know that I should have asked you first—it does belong to you—but it seems important to us all, for some reason, that he lives here too. He's already putting his things in the master suite. Have I messed up?"

"No. He should be here, for no other reason than to keep Bryce on her toes. She's not going to be happy with you when she finds out. So if I were you, I'd tell her that I did it. She'll be pissy, but it won't hurt you so badly when she walks away from you." Laura said that she could handle Bryce on this. "Perhaps you can. I've noticed that about you lately. You're stronger since coming here. I don't mean you just standing up to Bryce—you did that before—but you seem able to be physically stronger too. You've still not told her, have you?"

"No. I know that she needs to know, but I'm enjoying having her so close to me again. I'm afraid that when she does find out, she'll have me to every doctor on the planet. I don't want her doing that either." Bea could understand that too. Bryce would only want the best for her mother. "I never thought, when I was made an immortal, that it only meant that I'd be around for a long time, but I could still get sick. Cancer wasn't something that I'd counted on."

"No one counts on cancer, Laura. I'm sure that everyone that hears that they have it feels the same way that you do about it. It's a nasty business. I've seen firsthand what it can do to a person and their body." She'd watched a great many women pass from the ravaging disease. Her work at the hospice center had taken its toll on her. "You should tell her. I don't know what she would be able to do but knowing about it before too much longer will go a long way in having time to deal with this all."

"Tell Bryce what?" Noah sat down on the bench and smiled at the two of them. "My mom would be so proud of this. And jealous. She always wanted a nice sized garden, but she also didn't have much in the way of time to deal with it. Mom had all these social things that she was working on. Mostly for the new school when it had been built. You don't have cancer anymore, Laura."

The change in the subject was quick, and he stood up and stretched before making his way up the little path that she'd found yesterday. It led to the other garden, one that had been in much better shape, as well as size. As soon as Noah was out of sight, Bea looked at Laura's stunned face.

"Do you think he's right?" Bea told her that there wasn't any way for her to know if he was or not. But that didn't mean that she didn't have to tell Bryce if he was correct. "What did he do? I mean, obviously he knew that I had it. What do you suppose he did to make it so I don't anymore?"

"Now don't go getting your hopes up. He might not be able to tell that you even have it." Laura looked so crestfallen that Bea felt horrible for her words. "I'm sorry, Laura, but he's a dragon, not a physician. We'll have to wait and see."

"I'm going to go and talk to him." Laura stood up, and

41

Bea wanted to tell her to see a doctor first. "He might only be a dragon, but there is more to him than I think we see. Or that he allows us to see. At least for now."

Bea thought that she was right but didn't get the chance to say anything when Laura took off on the path. Whatever happened would happen, she knew this. And to interfere would mean that someone would have to pay.

Bryce would have taken the cancer away from her mom, Bea knew this. She also knew that Bryce would pay the price of her kind if she did. You could not be selfish as a witch. Never heal yourself, never do things for personal gain, and never, under any circumstances, were you to interfere with the death of a loved one. That, she knew, Bryce would overlook when it came to her mom's health. She supposed that was the main reason that she'd never gone to her and told her about her mom.

Putting the seeds from the leather pouch in the ground, Bea was excited to see them take root quickly and start to sprout. It wasn't her magic that did this, but that of the earth. And when she dug up the next row, careful of the plants already in the rich magical soil, Bea thought of her only son.

Austin had really been a good man—very confident in his abilities, and a great warlock. Teaching his only child, Austin had told her that Bryce was going to be the strongest witch ever born. He'd not only been correct about that, but also about the fact that he was going to die long before she became all that she could. It was why, two days before he'd been sentenced to death, he'd given his magic, all of it, to his daughter.

When Bryce met Noah, Bea remembered what Austin had told her about the magic. He said that she'd have to have a strong and powerful mate, someone that would be able to center her magic and her heart. There hadn't been anyone around that had touched that part of her granddaughter, only her and Laura. Now it seemed she had a mate to help.

Noah was exactly what Austin had predicted in a mate for Bryce. Not only was he very strong, an old and powerful dragon, but he had magic, more than enough to keep them all safe should it come to that. But when the magic of the faeries had gone to him as well, Bea had felt it, and knew that together the two of them, Bryce and Noah, would be enough to keep Bryce happy as well. Something that Bea didn't think Bryce had been a great deal of since Austin had been killed.

Now, she'd heard her granddaughter whistling the other morning. And she noticed that she looked for the dragon, seeking him out just to make him angry. She hadn't been able to do that yet; the man seemed to have the temperament to be calm no matter what was going on around him. He too looked happy. Bea decided to talk to Devon about his friend, to find out what he might know of him.

Bea saw Bryce before she did her. Stomping through the grass, she was also talking to herself—never a good sign. Putting the trowel away, Bea decided that she had better meet her halfway or Bryce might harm the little seedlings without realizing it. Almost as soon as she was close enough to her, she saw the mark on her face.

"What happened to you?" She tried to pull away. "Bryce, I demand that you tell me what has happened to you that would make such a mark on your face."

"It's nothing like you're thinking." Bea asked her what she might be thinking. "I have no idea, but this is from trying to hang a sheet of drywall by myself. I had it in my head that I could help out, and now I've not only dropped the piece I was holding on to, but two more sheets that were leaning against the wall have been damaged as well. I want the house finished now. I cannot wait one minute more."

The roar of magic soared over the ground. It not only knocked Bea off her feet, but it did Bryce as well. Whatever had happened, they both watched as the ground moved and rose up slightly as it headed for the house. She heard another sound, this one closer than before. And when the large dragon landed in front of them both, Bea laid her head down and waited to die.

When nothing moved, the ground around them still, Bea looked up to see the dragon staring at Bryce. She couldn't hear what she was saying to him, but whatever it was, she wasn't happy. The dragon, whom she could only assume was Noah, laid down on the ground, his large head at the feet of Bryce.

It was a sight to behold, the dragon being tamed by the witch. Bea was getting her hearing back, the loud sounds having temporarily blocking her from hearing for a moment or two. Bryce was taming the beast before her, telling him how much he'd frightened her and scared her grandmother. Not moving, not wanting to have any attention brought to her, Bea watched as the two of them come to terms with each other.

"You could have killed us both, you moronic fuck. And

don't you dare tell me again how you'd not. But you'd been protecting us. Did it look like we might need protecting from the earth when you came down here and blew your fire all over the place? I swear to you, Noah Farley, if one blade of herb is damaged on my grandmother's garden, I will put a fire to you that will make what you've done here look like a small campfire. Of all the stupid things you could have done." He must have said something to Bryce, because she smacked him on the nose as she continued. "I do not want to hear how you heard the roar and came to see what had happened. Most, anyone that I know, would have walked to us. Asked very politely what had happened. No, you had to come blowing your nasty breath all over everything until there is nothing left even for the animals to have."

"Bryce?" She looked in her direction, and Bea wasn't surprised when she came running over to her. She missed it then, her mate going from beast to man. That too was a beautiful thing, a man with so much magic letting his very small witch of a mate berate him when she was upset. "I'm all right, child. Leave the poor boy alone. Had you been in real trouble, would you have been happy to see him or not?"

"I was terrified that he was going to be hurt." Well, that wasn't what she had expected. "The way the magic came from the mountain top, I thought for sure someone had murdered him. Then he burnt the trees."

"They look fine to me."

Bryce fought with tears and finally gave in to them. Not reaching for her to comfort Bryce, she walked away when Noah took her granddaughter into his arms and held her.

45

The trees were fine for the most part. They were still healing, their bark coming green again, the leaves that had been singed greening up, like leaves in the spring. Walking to the house, she saw Laura sitting on the deck. Wondering how she'd gotten there, she sat beside her and asked her.

"Noah told me that he's able to heal me because I'm his mate's mother. And he said that I'd never have to worry about it again, cancer or anything else that a human might get. He told me that while I'm not dragon or witch, I will be just like the two of them in that I'll enjoy a long and healthy life with the rest of you." Laura looked at her then. "When the magic—he told me what it was—gathered on the hill, he told me where to go to hide. And to head to the house when I saw it. There is a tunnel, Bea, from the top of the mountain to the house, that he told me was there for me to use when I needed time to myself. He's even put me a little place up there, just for me to go and watch the animals."

"He's a good man. I thought him like our Austin, but I believe him to be so much more. If I were to have to choose someone to watch over Bryce, I could not have picked a better man than that one." Laura agreed. "Bryce was afraid for him. She yelled at him like a harpy for more than a few minutes, and he allowed it. I hate to keep comparing him to Austin, but he would have allowed you to do so for so long before he told you to leave him be. Noah, he just took it. Then when she cried, he held her like she was the most precious thing in the world to him."

"I believe that she is." Bea nodded. "I still have to tell her about the cancer. Noah said that it was only right that I did.

46

And he'll be with me, as he had healed me without talking to her. Noah told me that I hadn't had time to live — that by this time tomorrow, the cancer would have taken my mind and body, and it would have been too late."

~*~

Bryce didn't want to cry in front of anyone, but she'd been so afraid that not only had Noah been hurt, but that it had been because of her. When she was as finished as she could be, babbling to him about how she was mad at him, he lifted her chin up so that she could see his face.

"I'm a dragon." She rolled her eyes. "Yes, I know that you're aware of that, my dear. But I have a great many faeries, all of them in good standing, that will answer to you as well as me. Sometimes, I'm sure that they'll override me to do whatever it is you wish. But they heard your demand and were thrilled to have something they could do for you."

"I don't understand." He nodded, and she tried to pull away from him. "Noah, what are you talking about? And I know that faeries and dragons have a relationship. But what does that have to do with me?"

"They finished the house. And in order to fulfil your needs in the way you wanted, they all went there and finished every part of it." She thought about what she'd said. Bryce had wanted not just the house finished, but right now. Asking him what they'd done, he took her hand into his and they made their way back to the house. "I would imagine that they've seen what it is you want by searching your thoughts on how you expected it to look. And by doing so, and the time limit that you gave them, it took them all, all the forest of faeries, to do just as you wished."

"I was just aggravated by all the unfinished things going on in the house and things being in the way. I left the house in a huff because one of the sheets of drywall dropped and cut me. And two more were ruined too. I had forgotten how heavy drywall could be when it hits your head like that." Bryce put her fingers to her forehead and knew that the wound had healed. "Noah, I'm sorry that I yelled at you."

"I scared you. I can understand that." She told him that she didn't want him to understand, she wanted him to.... She didn't know what she wanted and told him that. "I understand that as well. There are many things that I want from you. Most of them have to do with laying you out on the bed upstairs and having my way with you. But there are a few things that have to do with you trusting me. Oh, and lots of sex. That will stop a lot of my thoughts too."

"I'm not sure that sex is the answer to everything." He said it was worth a shot. "No, it's not. Now, I need for you to explain a couple of things to me before we go inside. First of all, there was a call from the bank today. Why did you put me on your accounts?"

"You're my mate." She glared at him. "That's a good answer. You're my mate, and what I have is yours. What you have is yours as well. Though I have to tell you, what I have isn't all that much. An old plane that might be repossessed anytime now, and a crown that I don't even know where it is anymore."

"That's not even reasonably fair, is it?" Noah just smiled at her. "You keep doing that. Smiling and acting all charming when you think it'll get you whatever it is you want. Well, I have news for you, buddy—"

When he stiffened, she did as well. The change from man to dragon was quick, but she didn't have time to admire the way he'd done it. Something was coming. Something that, while not large, was powerful. Reaching into the earth and everything around them, she put a barrier between whatever it was and the two of them. The faerie queen, Dawn, rising up from the earth had her bowing at the waist and waiting for her to demand why the faeries, her faeries, had come to them.

"My lady, Lord Noah. I have never seen as much of you as I have in the past two days. All is well now?" Noah laughed and told her what had happened. "Yes, well, having one's home finished is something that I would want as well. Very good. I have been told that it is safe, and that with your own faeries, some have decided to stay with you within your walls."

"Thank you, my lady. But should you need them, I'll explain why they cannot stay." She said that it was up to them, but she was happy that they were there. "You have met my mate, Bryce. She is a powerful witch on her own. If you should wish to talk to her about something, I'm sure that she'd be happy to speak with you."

"I would." Embarrassed at how loudly she'd spoken, Bryce tried again. "I would love to talk to you, my lady. I have been in awe of the faeries, not only in my hometown but here as well. The gardens and the flowers about are the prettiest that I've ever seen."

"Thank you, my lady. That is high praise coming from

you. I have seen your gardens, those that you used at home. They are as rich and as plentiful as the ones you and your family are guarding here." Bryce thanked her again. "I have only come to ask that if the faeries become too much that you send them back. They all know that they are here only by the grace of your hospitality. Thank you again for taking so many into your household. They will serve you well, I think."

Bryce looked at Noah when he laughed after the queen left them. "Don't think that you're off the hook. You have yet to give me an answer that I believe. Why would a man such as yourself put my name, someone that he barely knows, on his accounts?"

"I told you, you're my mate." This time when he pulled her to his body, she felt his need, like a warm blanket that wrapped her snuggly up inside. And when his erection, hard and long, touched her at her pussy, she could no more have stopped the moan from spilling forth than she could have stopped her own beating heart. "I need you, Bryce. I want to taste you to see if the aromas that you have taste as amazing as they smell. I wish to nip you in places, only to sooth them with my tongue. To give you more than just a little pleasure, but to feel it, to have you come hard enough that my entire being feels it. My dragon smells you too, wants us to make love so that you belong to us and no other. Erase the others from your body, men that came before us."

The kiss wasn't anything but a claiming. He possessed her with his mouth, molded her body to fit tightly with his. And when he lifted her, her legs wrapped around him as if they had done this a million times, letting Noah have her as if

50

she truly did belong to him.

"Noah." He kissed her again, savagely this time, his mouth searing a mark from her lips to her throat. And when he bit down, tearing into her heated flesh, she cried out with a release that instead of satisfying even a small part of her, made her crave and need more.

Bryce didn't remember why she'd said his name. Or even, for that matter, if she'd been about to ask him a question, like why didn't he take her now, or if she was going to ask him to stop. Nothing in the world could have prepared her for the man holding her. And no amount of magic could make her walk away from him.

Noah backed from her, and Bryce wanted to beg him. But when he turned into his dragon again, lifting her up with him as he took to the skies, she clung to his beast as the house grew smaller, the trees looking like tiny sticks. Then they landed on the mountain top. He was man again, and this time he wasn't pulling away but shredding her clothing from her body.

Touching his body was all she could think about. His skin was hot—his muscles rippled under her fingers like he was a running river, warmed by the sun. She needed him. Bryce hadn't ever needed anything in all her life, not food or water, like she did this man. And she knew that she would never again need anything but him.

He took her hard, his cock already filling her even before they were on the ground. He spoke to her, his words in a language that she'd not heard before. Not that it mattered. For some reason she knew that he was telling her that he loved her, and Bryce knew that she loved him.

"Say it." His thick cock was making her needier while he stilled deep inside of her. Bryce looked at him, wondering what he'd said. "Tell me. Tell me that you love me, Bryce. Please. I want to hear you say the words."

"I love you. But I'm not going to be easy."

His grin made her want to smack him, but when he kissed her then moved inside of her, she screamed out how much she loved him even as he bit down on her shoulder.

Bryce had heard the term "My eyes rolled to the back of my head," but she had never experienced it until now. Her body spun around, and she was sure her head came off, only to be set back on upside-down. None of this really happened, of course, but it made her feel as if she'd been turned inside out, run over, and her fingers stuck into a life socket all at once. And she had never felt better in her entire life.

Then she released. Her hair came, her nose, as well as her toes. Every part of her body, even parts that she was sure had been stuck on just for the thrill of the release, hit her. Screaming, a mundane term for how she had said Noah's name, wrenched from her mouth, tearing at her throat so harshly that she was sure that she'd never speak again. And when he came too, his body emptying into her, Bryce came again. Her body bowed up from the ground and her nails dug deeply into his back, holding on so that she'd not scatter to the winds. Bryce fell back to the earth and simple died, she was sure of it.

Waking, Bryce found herself in their bed. Moving to see if she was alone, she moaned loudly when she realized how sore she was. She supposed it was better than she'd thought.

If she'd died, then they could never have that kind of sex again. And she so wanted to do that over and over.

Finding herself alone in the room, she went to the bathroom thinking that a nice hot shower would make some of the kinks go away. As soon as she turned the water on, she heard her name called from the bedroom. It was Noah.

"Devon called while you were out. He wants us to come over for dinner. He said that he has a couple of things that he'd like to talk over with you." She said that she could do that and asked if he knew what it might be. "No, he only said that he needed to get a couple of things cleared up, and he was happy that we've gotten the house taken care of. I'm not sure how he figured it out, but I told him that it looked great."

"Does it?" Noah laughed and said that it looked fantastic. "Grandma will be happy too, then. As well as my mom. I think she's been itching to make something in her new domain since she found out that there was a big kitchen. Are you going to live here with me?"

"Yes. If you would allow it." She nodded. "What's the matter? Besides being very sore. Has something happened that has upset you?"

"Not that I'm aware of. But I'm not sure where that wanton woman came from on the mountain. That wasn't me." He laughed. "I'm serious. I have never had sex that...I guess you could call it violently before. It was fantastic, but never have I ever had my head spin around."

"I'm glad that I could help you out with that."

She held his hand as they made their way down the stairs. Her grandmother and mom were waiting for them. And with one look, she knew that something had happened.

Chapter 4

Noah waited until the women of the household were finished talking before he spoke. He'd been waiting for some time now, about forty-five minutes. But he knew that as soon as they were finished with their plans, they'd let him speak.

"I'd not count on it, my lord." He grinned at William when he landed on his shoulder. "Do you suppose that they ever take the advice of others? They seemed to also be loud in their talking."

Noah had made a comment that the women were very loud. And that had them turning on him so quickly that he had to remind himself that he was a dragon and much larger than them. After that, he'd decided that he'd not only keep his mouth shut but would wait. Glancing at the large grandfather clock in the room, he realized that he'd been wrong. It had been an hour and forty-five minutes. He needed to get their attention.

He'd always been good at whistling, and he had an attention grabbing one that could break glass should he do it long enough. But when he did it now, it had the exact result that he'd hoped for. They all three turned to him and glared. He supposed that he should have waited a bit longer.

"I have a question. Well, several, but this one needs to be answered for me to be able to keep up. The WC, Witches' Council, is made up of three witches—none of them terribly smart, and all men. Why is that?" Bea winked at him as she sat on the couch beside him. "I'm pretty smart, if you're thinking that I won't understand."

"It's not that." Laura sat down too as she continued. "They have always hated that I'm Bryce's mother. And when she got her okay to be a full-fledged witch, working with them instead of against, I guess they hoped that Bryce would want to rid herself of the dead weight—what they called me—instead of what she chose as her one rule."

"So, this trial of sorts, this is to try another way of getting rid of you." Laura nodded. "And why would it matter to them one way or the other if Bryce has you as dead weight? I don't believe for a moment that you are, but they should have a reason, shouldn't they?"

"Oh, they do. They don't like Mom. They think she's a busybody and holds me back from my full potential." When Bryce sat across from him, nearer the fireplace that was unlit, he wanted to get her and have her sit on his lap. But this was serious. "The day before I graduated with honors, they tried to say that I'd cheated, that my mom had put me up to it."

Bea laughed, and he looked at her.

"It's doubtful that anyone, for a great many years, will try that one again. Not only did Bryce prove to them that she'd not cheated, but she took the man to...I guess you could call it to task." Bea laughed harder. "The man accusing her had been pitted against Bryce, because his thinking was that no woman would be stronger than a warlock. Anyway, I do believe that they're still picking pieces of him out of the carpet. I told them to put in hardwood floors, but no one listened to me. They do now, thanks wholly to Bryce, but—"

"Grandma, you're rattling on about things that Noah doesn't need to know." Bea patted him on the arm and said she'd fill him in later. Bryce continued, but now she had a tone to her voice that made him think she wasn't happy with either of them. "They're saying that my mother killed a man unjustly. And that I cannot represent her in front of the council."

"She didn't kill anyone. I'll never believe that she did." Laura turned to him and smiled. "You did it? You killed someone? Christ, now I have to know how."

"He was trying to have his unwanted way with me. Not sexually, though that would have been so much worse. Douche head was trying to get me to let him experiment on my body." Laura laughed. "The man thought that I should allow him to enlarge my breasts and other parts of my body so that he could touch them. He was doing an experiment, he told me, trying to figure out if the feelings were the same. I turned him down. I thought I had an ample enough bosom."

"And I take it that it didn't end after you said no." She shook her head and glanced at Bryce. "Did your daughter protect your honor?"

"Oh no, I killed him. But it was the how I did it that has made the council upset. You see, when my husband was killed, they assumed that I'd follow him, the way the coven we were in at the time did it. If you didn't die of a broken heart, then you never truly loved each other." He said that dragons did that as well but weren't made to do it. "Yes, well, I loved Austin, but not enough to die with him. I had family support, and that kept me going. Also, Bryce and Bea gave me a bit more magic to add to what Austin, Bryce's father, had given me. It was enough to not only kill the man, but also more than enough that his death wasn't easy. I was angry myself, as you can well understand."

"Yes. I understand. And this man, the one you keep calling douche head, he was going to help you along with joining your mate?" Laura nodded, then shook her head. "He was there, but there was more to it, correct?"

"When they came for my mom after he—his name was David—was dead, they said that I had to kill my mom in the form of payment to his family. Since I'd already told them that my mother was the one person in the world that I'd never give up, they decided to make an example of me. That didn't work out so well either. And now, they're coming here to collect." He asked what they were hoping to collect. "You. They know that I've taken a mate, that we've become one. However, what they don't know, and I hope you plan to make them aware of, is that you're a dragon."

It took Noah several seconds to realize what she was saying. She wanted him to show himself to be a dragon, and maybe warn them off. Noah was still laughing when William went to sit on the shoulder of Bryce, something that he'd never seen him do before.

"Yes, I'll do this. Gladly. But what if they don't care that I'm a dragon, and try to take me anyway? I'm sure that they're going to try." Bryce said that he could count on it. "Then what? Do I get myself in trouble too?"

"No. You burn one of them. They won't die, not this group, but by hurting one of them, to prove that you and I aren't a couple to fuck with, then they'll back off." He asked her if she knew this or hoped that it would make them back off. "I'm hoping. They've been chasing this dream of taking my mom for some time now. And I want it to end."

"They wish to control you, my lady." Everyone turned to look at William. "I have seen their minds. Nasty places, if you should like to know. They know that you are stronger than them. And should you wish it, you could take over and make the rules. They think that you won't make the rules to suit yourself, as they have done, but that your rules will benefit all witches."

"I don't want to run the council." He asked Bryce why not. "Because it turns a person into something else. A man that I knew and admired was put on that thing, and now he's starting to be no better than the rest of them. No, I don't want to be something that I'm not."

"Black was always as you know him, worse now that he has some power. He hid it in his head that you and he could become close. So that he could be the voice of reason when it would benefit him. And now that he's where he is, high man on the council, he's decided to use the power that he was given to kill you." Bryce looked at him, and then at her grandmother. "If they can control you, by any means, they'll kill those that mean the most to you. After that, they feel that they will be in a better position to make you do as they wish."

"I don't understand. I already dislike Kurt. How does he think this is going to get me to trust him?" William said that grief can make a person do odd things. "Yes, I know that too. So, their plan is to take my mate and hold him over my head. And if that doesn't work, they'll more than likely kill him too, if they can, and let me think that it was some sort of accident."

"Your family will be targeted as well should you prove to be less than helpful to them. There will be trouble, not just for Lord Noah, but for us and the faerie queen as well."

Noah knew that if called upon to help, all the faeries of the world would come to their aid. He just hoped it never came to that.

Noah watched Bryce think. She was very quiet, unlike him, who would toss out idea after idea. She didn't fidget either, just sat there looking relaxed while she went through more ideas than the council would ever think of — or for that matter, think that she'd ever think of — and then discarded them.

"There are others that we can call on, Bryce." She nodded and looked at Bea when she said more to her granddaughter. "There is a governing council that oversees the WC. They're very difficult to get in touch with, but I do believe that one of them told Bryce once that he would be at her beck and call. She saved him, you see."

"I didn't save him. I simply told him that he'd be better served in not marrying Janice. She wasn't what he wanted in a mate." Bryce shook her head. "Most people that met him would have known that it wasn't women that he was attracted to. That's all I did, just pointed out that he might want to pursue that avenue before marrying the first woman that he slept with."

Noah loved his new family. They were witty, fun, and a group of the most beautiful women that he'd been around in a long time. And they made him feel like he could take on the world. He wasn't sure why he felt that when he was with them, but he did feel that if they ever needed him, he could slay...well, slay another dragon should they need for him to.

"I have an idea. But it's going to take some help from William." The little man puffed out his chest and told Bryce that he'd do anything for her. "You might want to wait until you hear what it is first. You might just want to take that back."

"Never, my lady. I am here to serve you." She nodded and looked at Noah. If she was asking for permission, he couldn't give it to her. William now belonged solely to Bryce. "He will have his own faerie now, my lady. I was with him only until you showed up. Not to say that I have not enjoyed my time with him, but he will need a female faerie, to balance him out. As I will do for you."

"Okay, but if you don't want to do this, then that's fine too. And before too much more time goes by, I want you to get to know Fred. He's my animal to call." She looked at Noah again. "Unless you'd like the job. Fred has wanted to retire someplace warm for a long time now. If you would be my animal to call, then that would make things easier for us both."

"Yes, I'll do that for you." He had no idea what that meant, other than he'd be there for her. And since that was his plan anyway, he thought he could do this as well. "What do I have to do?"

Before she could tell him why she was smiling, he realized that he should have asked that before he said he'd do it. His body felt like it was humming. That his dragon was somehow being hurt. And before he could guess what was happening to him, the pain took his breath away and called his dragon.

~*~

Bea couldn't stop laughing, and it seemed that the more Noah glared at her, the harder she wanted to laugh. His dragon hadn't found it very humorous either when he'd been ordered out of the house an hour ago. They were separate beings now, man and beast, and Bea hadn't expected that to happen.

"You can put him back." Noah growled at Bryce. "You said you'd do it. It's not my fault that you just jumped right in and said—"

"You at least warned William. Why wasn't I given the same warning?" Noah asked Bryce what she said when she mumbled. "I can't hear you. Did you just tell me this way was more fun? I'll have you know that we'll never get those scratches out of the floor. And the fireplace is ruined."

"Oh, you sound like an old woman." Bryce's reply made Bea laugh all the harder. Noah sort of did act and sound like an old woman. But Bryce wasn't finished with him yet. "We can have the faeries fix things back. Will that make poor little Noah feel better?"

He growled again just before he leapt at Bryce. As they rolled around on the floor, Bea made her way to the kitchen. Laughter rang through the house, and Bea thought that the sound would make a wonderful doorbell sound just as the infernal thing started ringing. Going to the door, Bea jerked it open before the person on the other side rang it again.

"Yes?" The woman looked at her, then to her left. Bea knew who was there — Noah had come to see who it was as well. Just as she was going to ask the woman again who she might be, she looked at Noah.

"They told me that you were the best there is at figuring it out. My brother, he was killed several weeks ago, and the police keep telling me that it was suicide. It wasn't. Parker would never do anything like that."

Noah invited the woman in and led her into the parlor as she continued to talk. Bea made her way to the kitchen again. Asking for some tea and something to go with it had every creature in the room vying for a chance to put something on the plates. She watched as a high pitch of buzzing and talking accompanied the little creatures, arguing over what was the proper way to put things together. But as soon as Bryce walked into the room, it was as if a spell had been put upon them to freeze where they were. The only movement was their wings.

"We have a guest, as I'm sure that you're aware of. And since she was able to step over the threshold, you also must be aware that she has no desire to hurt anyone in this house." Bea hadn't known that was there, that little bit of protection, but was glad for it. "All right. She is tired and upset and flittering about in this room is not making her welcome. I want you to figure out who will be in charge of the kitchen area, and for that person to hire as many of you as they wish for this room. After that, I'll take requests for the rest of the household."

Bea was impressed. Her granddaughter had taken to being in charge like a pro. And when one of the faeries shifted from their tiny self to a little elderly woman, she knew that they had a cook now.

"I'm simply called Flower, my ladies. I will organize and take care that the kitchen is well stocked and good meals come from here." Bryce thanked her. "I should like to have me four helpers, if you will please allow it. I might need more, but we can take care of that as we go, if you please."

"Perfect. Now, we'll need a butler. William will be my faerie from now on, and I will have Noah's dragon as my animal to call. You all are aware of what we women are, so if you wish to not stay, that is perfectly fine with me. Also, we will need garden workers, as many as wish to work with the flowers and such. And the rest...well, I guess we'll work those out as we go."

A young man—more than likely older than both her and Bryce put together, Bea realized—was dressed in a lovely suit, as well as the whitest gloves she'd ever seen. He asked to be called Melville. It was from a story that he had heard once, and he loved the name.

"Good. Now, take the tray of cookies and tea and such into the parlor. From now on, please ask before we take something. They might not have a wish to harm us, but that doesn't mean we want to make them comfortable. But then I'm sure as butler, Melville, you'll be able to tell when they'll wear out their welcome fast or not." Melville said that he would, bowed to them and took the tray. Bryce looked at her. "Grandma, I'm sure you could use some help in the gardens. Please do take a few with you so that you're not alone. I don't know that anyone would want to harm you, but you never know."

"I will, darling. And I must say, you're doing very well as queen of the castle." Bryce stuck her tongue out at her and and Bea laughed. "There she is. I knew that the real Bryce couldn't stay hidden for long."

She went with her to the parlor. Noah was comforting the woman on the chair, and just shook his head when she asked if things were all right. When they were all seated, Bea served the tea and cookies while the woman, her name was Hannah Westin, was wiping her tears.

"Hannah has a brother, Parker, who was found dead five weeks ago of an apparent suicide. Since then he's been cremated without her permission, and his ashes have been returned to her. The problem is, she can't get anyone to help her figure out why he did it, nor where his body was found. All the police are telling her is that it's a rough side of town, and that she should be happy that anyone found him at all." Bryce asked why she didn't believe them. "Ah...well, there has been a time, recently, that the entire town thought that the station house was corrupt. And that they're hiding things, such as the death of her brother, because of something that they did to him. Parker was a good man—studying for the priesthood, as a matter of fact."

"And what are they saying to you about the place, other than it's in a terrible location?" Hannah said that was all she could get. "And the newspaper. What did they print up about it?"

She pulled out a file with papers in it and handed it to Bryce. Hannah said that was all they had written. That they'd printed almost word for word what the police had told her.

"That a man had been found in an undetermined area of the town and that he had committed suicide. How on earth can they say an undetermined area? That's saying that they don't have any idea where he was found. Idiots." Bea noticed that Hannah was getting fired up, and a little of her sadness was gone. "I want to find out what happened. I need to know. My brother was all I had in the world, and now they're saying this crap about him. Please, I'll pay you whatever you want. Just please tell me the truth. That's all I ever wanted."

Noah looked over the newspaper clippings and asked several questions about them. Bryce sat there, not really looking at anyone, but Bea had a feeling that she could tell what everyone had said and knew where everything was in the room. But for now, she was working on something. This was how she did it best.

"I'll go and look for you." Hannah thanked Noah. "Don't thank me yet. Whatever I find out, it might not be anything you want to hear. Are you going to be prepared for that?"

"Yes. As I said, I need to know what happened. If it turns out that he killed himself, then I'll have to live with that. But if he didn't, I want to know why the police and everyone around me is trying their best to cover it up." Noah nodded and looked over at Bryce. "I'll pay you whatever you wish."

"That won't be necessary. We'll do this for you so long as you believe us when we tell you the answers." She nodded. "Please, I need to hear you say it, Hannah. That will be payment enough if you simply let us find you some answers, and then believe that we're not going to lie to you."

"I know that. I've been asking around, and they say that you're the best at figuring out crimes. And you've brought justice for a lot of people." Hannah stood up and put out her hand. Bea thought that she was asking for a handshake, but she had something in her palm. "This is off of a shirt that was in his room. Also, I have a few pieces of his hair from his brush. I don't know what you'll need, but I didn't think it would hurt to bring it to you."

The plastic Baggie held what she could see was a piece of a soft material. She'd bet anything that it was from his pajamas. That was something that would have the most scents on it, even after it had been washed. She couldn't see the hair from where she was, but both Noah and Bryce looked it all over. They'd find him, and what had happened to him too.

After Hannah was shown out, Bea went to the kitchen again. Dinner was about to start, and since the lady and lord of the house were on the chase, she decided to see what mischief she could find to get into. Just as she was thinking about what she could get up to, Laura asked her if she wanted to take a walk. That, she decided, was better than anything.

She and Laura had gotten along as soon as Austin

introduced her to the family. She was brilliant. Not only was she smart, but there was a light about her that made you smile no matter your mood. And she loved Bea's son as much as she did. That, Bea thought, was also why she loved the girl like her own child. Laura had believed in Austin—not always in what he was doing, but that he'd give whatever it was its best.

"I almost forgot—I've been thinking of having a little tea party. I don't know when. Later in the year perhaps, or the next. We need to settle up." Laura asked if she was going to make it a yearly event, as she had before. "Yes, I thought that as well. With so much going on, it'll give us something to look forward to. I'm going to let Noah know too. I don't want him to feel left out, do you? Anyway, we'll talk about it later. Just keep reminding me about it, will you, Laura?"

"I will. And you're right about that. He's a good man." Laura said that he was everything she'd ever hoped for her daughter. "Yes. She and him, they're matched very well. And they don't get all bothered when they're joking around either. I haven't laughed as hard as I did today when she called his dragon. But I will admit, I didn't think that he'd be separated from him that way, did you?"

"No. I mean, that's a good thing, I think. If he's hurt or taken, as she thinks might happen, being able to call his dragon would save his life if he is unable to do it." Bea hadn't thought of that but was glad that someone mentioned it. Whatever happened, as far as she was concerned, they'd have each other's back. And for that, she was happy.

If the council wanted to get rid of Laura, they'd be in

deeper shit than they thought they might be if Bryce took over. And even though she said that she didn't want to, Bea knew that she'd do a wonderful job if she did. There were too many rules that weren't fair, and even more things that had been going on lately that she thought were shady. Bea hoped that it came to a head.

For two reasons really. One, she knew that Bryce, and now Noah, would take care of it. And the second thing, she wanted to watch. While she was still a good person, it made her feel good when the bad guy got what was coming to him and his ass was kicked hard. And in this, she had no doubt that they would.

Chapter 5

The area that they'd found wasn't really what he'd consider to be in a *bad* place. But it wasn't all that good of an area either. It was just a place where the younger generation hadn't come in and noticed that it needed to be upgraded. Or downgraded when they went in and made everything all retro. It depended on how one looked at it, he supposed.

To him, he loved the old blended with the new. It was a balancing act, yes, but he thought that wood — anything made of any kind of wood — was his favorite. And Noah saw no reason that it couldn't be paired with a lovely lamp made of glass and steel. But no carpet. That he hated more than he did those nasty Brussels sprouts that his mom used to make him eat. Full of vitamins, she told him. Yuck.

The building that the death occurred in was powered and it had running water. The rooms hadn't been swept nor the cobwebs bothered with, but it was in reasonable shape, at least for a building that supposedly hadn't been used in the last twenty or so years. Not so on the upper level. That's where he and Devon were now, as Bryce checked out the other buildings.

"Something happened here, but I don't think it was the death of Parker, do you?" Devon said that he didn't think so either. "I'm smelling a great deal of something, but I can't quite put my finger on what it is. Old, that's all I can figure out. Not that it's old and worn out, but something from when you and I were younger."

"I agree. It smells like herbs. Perhaps your wife can tell better what it might be." Yeah, she'd be able to tell them. She'd been helpful a great deal on this case. It made him happy that they could work together so well in their life together. "What is it she's looking for out there anyway?"

"She said that she could feel that someone had used magic around here. When I asked her if it had been a shifter, and she said that it was a different kind of magic. Other than black and white, I had no idea there was a different sort of magic, did you?" Devon laughed and said that he wasn't sure that even black and white would have been different to him. "Yes, well, she'll get to the bottom of this."

When she joined them in the room they were in, she paused in the doorway. He knew that she could smell it too and would more than likely know what it was. He and Devon waited. Whatever was going on, he thought she was better at this than he'd be. There wasn't a body for him to look over, of course, but the whole thing, that was stumping him.

"He wasn't killed here—I'm sure that you've figured

that out." Noah said that he had. "And — and this might be just me — but I don't think that he's dead at all. There are just too many things that I'm finding around his *death* that aren't adding up. Like the building out there, the one that I was looking at. It has his scent in it more than this place does. And someone, some kind of odor is there that I just can't place but know of. Like, I don't know, drugs or something. On top of that, I'm smelling fresh food and drinks. Could be that someone is staying there and they're being fed."

"You said he died someplace else. Where do you think that happened, if at all? Or are you saying that you think that's his scent out there in that building, and someone else's here?" Bryce nodded at Devon when he asked. "You think he's alive, don't you? Okay, let us all work them out and see if we can come up with answers. If not, then we'll dig deeper. But the first thing I'd like to know is, why do you think that Parker isn't dead?"

"Would you believe me if I told you that the man that they killed didn't know who Parker Westin was? At least not his name, anyway." Devon said that he'd believe anything she told him, and Noah said that he would as well. "Okay, the man they had hanging here, they thought they had Westin. This person, his name hasn't come to me yet, told them that over and over as they murdered him. What I don't understand is why they killed this man when they didn't have the right guy. The man, whoever he was, he didn't die here — that's what I mean too. I think he was taken someplace else, and died before they could figure out he wasn't going to make it. Also, and this is the strangest part, over there behind that pile

73

of wood, I'm feeling the real Westin. Like he was watching what they were doing to this guy. Or he wasn't conscious. That's the one I'm thinking is what really happened."

Devon nodded, but still looked confused when he spoke to Bryce. "So, this other person dies on the way to someplace? More than likely, you think a hospital or someone to keep him living? Then when he dies, they bring him back here to dump his body." She nodded. "Okay, that's plausible. I can see that happening. Then what happened when they figured out it wasn't Westin?"

"They had nothing to go on other than he had his identification. Westin's, I think. I don't know how he did it. Maybe he stole it or something." Bryce shrugged as she continued. "Whatever happened to this other person, it wasn't Westin that they killed."

"You think that this other person perhaps stole Westin's wallet, and that is what got him screwed up?" Bryce told him that could be it exactly. "Okay, so where is he now?"

"The better question would be, why was he supposed to be murdered so violently? His name was Ronald Dentin, by the way. Having magic is the only way this is going to be solved; you are aware of that, correct?" Noah asked her how the man had been killed. "They hung him here, pelting him with questions that of course he didn't know the answers to, as they cut into his body. Mostly with knives, but they also used a nail gun and a saw. That's why *Westin* was cremated. If Hannah had seen what this man looked like, she'd have known he suffered. And on her part, she would have known it wasn't her brother."

"Then perhaps—not that I'd wish this other man to have suffered—but that means that her brother is still out there." Bryce just looked at him and Devon looked confused. "What am I missing?"

"He might not be this goody good guy that his sister thinks he is. I mean, if these guys thought that he knew something and were willing to kill for it, then it stands to reason that it couldn't have been good." Devon looked around, and so did Noah. "This is not a place where you would bring a priest to ask for forgiveness. There isn't anyone around. No businesses, and there was electricity to this place. They had this scoped out before they came here."

Noah went to the place where the real Westin would have been. He still didn't have a body, but with a living person, if he was still alive, he could work from there. Putting his hands into the dirt, he could barely read anything in it. Then Bryce came up behind him and put her hands on his shoulders. It was like his body was using some of her magic.

"Westin wasn't conscious when they finished with the other man. As soon as he woke from a nasty blow to the head, he saw the other man hanging there still. Thinking that they were still around, he got down on his knees and puked before he prayed." Noah glanced at the nasty pile that was in the corner from where they were. "He's still alive as of nine in the morning two days ago. He came to make sure that the other man had been found. He's in hiding."

"What does he know, can you tell that?" Noah said that he couldn't, but he knew where the man was hiding out. "Please tell me that it's not someplace out in the open."

75

"It's not. And you're going to love this." He stood up, dusting his hands off, and looked behind Devon. "Hello. You must be Parker Westin. We were sent to find you by your sister."

The man was dirty and looked like he'd not slept for the entire time that he'd been missing — or in this case presumed dead. Sobbing that he was happy to hear that Hannah was all right, he nearly sagged with relief when Noah told him that he'd help him. But they needed to know why he was here in the first place.

"Ronald Dentin called me in a frenzy. He said that he'd gotten himself into a pickle. And that's the way he said it too — he was in a pickle. When I got here, I could tell that he was coming down from something, and he asked me if I had any money on me. I didn't, and I tried to tell him that I couldn't help him until he got himself cleaned up. And I'd help him with that as well." They made their way down the stairs when Parker stopped. "I met him right there. He was doing something, but I wasn't able to get close enough to figure it out. But then he told me flat out that he wasn't going to get help, that he liked being high. Then he took off for the upper levels."

"Was there anyone up there when you got there?" Parker told Bryce that he'd not seen anyone. "And how did you end up behind the wood pile? I mean, you weren't there, were you, when the men showed up?"

"Oh no. I didn't know anything about men until I woke up and saw what had happened to that poor man. Ronald wanted drugs, he told me, and I told him again that I had no

76

money. That was when everything went out for me. It wasn't until I woke that I saw that he'd been...they made him suffer, didn't they?" Parker asked if they had any water, and when they went to get a bottle, Bryce asked him some questions. "The reason that I ended up behind the wood? I don't know for sure, but I'd guess that Ronald took me there. Perhaps so I'd not be hurt more."

"When you first came to us, you were told that your sister was looking for you. And you were thankful that she was all right too. Why? What made you think that she'd be in trouble?" Noah closed his trunk and handed the bottle to Parker. And when he did, he touched the man's fingers. "And why didn't you contact her when you were all right? I mean, for all you knew, they could have been after Ronald all along. Right?"

"I don't know what you're implying." Parker's voice got hard, suspicious even. It put both him and Bryce on alert. Even Devon seemed to understand that this wasn't right. When Parker backed up about as far as he could get and still be in the building, Bryce took a step forward and put out her hands. Whatever she'd done, Parker was aware of it. "Let me go this minute. This is no way to treat a man of the cloth."

"You aren't as sweet as you've let on, are you? I mean, your job as a priest is just a cover. You're actually dealing drugs right under the noses of those that are trying their best to get them off the very streets that you work on—a good cover." When he tried to move, no doubt to run, Noah realized that Bryce was holding him with her magic. "Your poor sister doesn't have a clue what sort of person you are, does she? I mean, to hear her talk about you, it's almost as if you're not the same person."

"You're barking up the wrong tree. I haven't any idea what you're talking about." Noah asked Devon to call the police. "What are you doing now? Did I not tell you that they're after me?"

"No, you failed to mention that. Who was it that Ronald took your place for? Was it one of your sellers? Perhaps an angry customer of yours?" The curse words that started to spew from the "man of the cloth's" mouth made all three of them laugh. Devon said that the police were on their way. "I do believe that you're going to have a lot of questions to answer, Parker. Like that little business that you have going over there in that building. What happened — did poor Ronald walk in there? Find out what you were doing?"

"You're in so much trouble here. I work for some very important people." Noah asked him if he meant God. "No, you moronic fuck. I work for some people that have names like Shark, Knife, and a few others. You do not want to mess with me. I'm telling you right now, you're going to wish the fuck that you listened to me when I warned you off."

"You see, I don't warn off easily. I'm the type of person that goes in full blast. And then when I catch my man? Well, I have all kinds of fun." He started cursing again when the sirens sounded closer to them. "My goodness. You sure do have a way with words, don't you?"

"You're going to regret this. I swear to you that I'm going to make sure that I get your names, and I'm going to send someone to take you out."

The cops came into the room and seemed to know Bryce. They also knew Devon, but were a little more intimidated with him. Someone having money would do that — or perhaps the fact that he was a dragon too. Either way, they were very happy to have Father Parker in their custody.

"Hello Bryce. It's been a while since we worked together here in my part of the world. But this guy, we've been trying to find him for a few months. And when there was that body, we had to work fast in not having the sister find out about him. She didn't have any idea what her big brother was up to, I don't think." Bryce introduced Noah to the police, telling him how they'd called her in when they'd had a crime they couldn't solve. All of them were happy that Bryce had a mate, and a couple of them looked crestfallen. He had to laugh when one of the men asked Bryce if she was happy with the arrangements.

"Yes, very much so. Sorry, Toby, but that's the way it goes." The poor kid looked like he'd just lost his all-day sucker. "But you might be seeing a good deal of me around now. We've purchased the castle in Manningtree. It's very lovely."

~*~

Bryce explained what they'd found out when the sister, Hannah, had asked them to find him. Arnold, the first officer on site, said that he'd been the one that suggested that she find Noah. That was before he knew that Bryce was in town too.

"I felt really bad for her. And lying to her about her brother just didn't set right either. I wanted to tell her that he was still alive and that we were looking for him, but then she might want us to find him for her. Or, if he contacted her, she might tell him that we were out looking for him still." Parker was taken away, still screaming that they'd regret this. "We have his boss on speed dial. He's forever making a mess for us to clean up. About Ronald—he was a small-time dealer who mostly filled his own nose with the shit that he would get from Parker. The best we can figure it, they had a nice fight, and Parker called in some of his goons and killed him. Then Parker faked his own non-involvement in Dentin's death to keep doing what he'd been doing. The church is going to be happy to have him gone as well."

Bryce showed the police the building that she'd been looking at. There wasn't any need for her to go in to know that meth was being made there. Anyone that got close enough would have been able to tell. Arnold Banks, Manningtree's constable, said that they'd had someone on it for several months now. They'd been waiting to catch someone higher up, namely Parker.

After they cleaned up the mess that had been made, mostly for evidence from both places, Noah, Devon and herself walked to their car. It was going to be up to the police to talk to Hannah. They'd know what to say and what couldn't be said. But, Arnold told them, they'd be getting full credit for the collar. Without them, she knew that they'd have still had this on their books.

"Hey, I have a question for the three of you. I have a few unsolved cases that I'd like to have gone before I retire next year." Bryce asked him what sort of crimes. "Well, mostly like this one. Drugs or murder, but not too many of the latter. Then I have one that has been there for only a few days. Insurance company wants me to see if the death in a house fire was just that. I've barely had time to even ask to have his autopsy done, much less go over the house. The house has been boarded up, by the insurance company again, and the family is driving them crazy to collect so that they can move on. I'm worried if I mess this up, there will be a lot of people not getting a pay off."

"You think that its suspicious?" Arnold nodded at her and told her that was why he wasn't rushing it. "And this house, the man was in it when it went up? I'm assuming that the body is still in cold storage."

"Yes. They had an empty casket at his funeral so that he could be kept for me to go over. But like I said, I have so many things to go over that I've not had a great deal of time." Noah asked if there were that many murders in this town. "No, not at all. But when you have five counties for our morgue, then things get a little behind."

She could see that. And in a bigger town, like Essex, it would be even worse. They agreed to take on the cases on a case to case load. There was no point in them getting as overloaded as the department was if they didn't have to. Bryce was happy for the work.

"This is something that I did in the States, working on cases. I had this detective that would always find something to bitch about, but worse with me." Bryce asked Noah if he had quit. "Not to hear them tell it. I'm still on their roster, but it was getting to be too much. Not really the stress of it but trying hard not to use too much of myself to get one solved. Then there was the fact that my dragon needed out more. It's extremely difficult to fly, even on cloudy days, when there are so many people with drones around."

Making their way back home, she studied the file that they'd picked up. There were pictures in the file, along with a log of calls made to the department by the family. One person that kept showing up was Howard Carter.

Howard had been married to Mr. Krupps's daughter. But they had long since divorced and had quite a few rows since them. One in particular was about two weeks before the fire, when there was some dispute about money. It had turned violent in the local pub. Bryce asked if they could run by the house.

"Sure, it's about on the way home anyway." Bryce had forgotten that Devon had lived here his whole life and got them there in just a few minutes. "Christ, that was a horrible fire."

Most of the roof was gone, as well as two of the walls. One of the other ones was being held up by a pipe leaning into it. The fourth one was just fine other than the windows were blown out. Getting out, they walked around while she read off the findings that had been noted after the fire had been put out.

"Electric has been shut off, but it says that the garage is still with power. That way, if a copper, just what it says, could make it out here in the evening, then he'd be able to have a torch." She looked in the gaping hole that had been a window as she continued. "This would be the kitchen. It didn't start in here. You can see how the fire burned less in here. Had it been the starting place, it would have been totaled."

"There's an electrical cord here." Noah kicked it around before turning to follow it to the garage. When he stopped and turned to her, he looked confused. "I just thought of something. It was boarded up. I mean, he did say that, didn't he? If so, then why are the boards on this side all taken off?"

Good question. As they researched more, they found an old fridge in the garage that had soot damage to it, and shelves of the same sort of canned food. It would be a mystery meal when opening them, as all the labels were burnt off, and a couple of them looked like they might have been contaminated. They were fat with poisons.

The more they looked around, the more they realized that it wasn't just some homeless person living there, but Howard Carter. And he was also working on the home. Some materials were stacked up behind the garage with a tarp over them, and Howard had signed for them. The bill was net ninety days. The man, they assumed, was banking on having the insurance money before three months' time. But why fix up the house?

Calling the police seemed like the best thing to do, and when they arrived, not only were there two of them, but they were in their personal vehicles with no lights. Devon knew these men as well. It seemed that he had an in with everyone in his little burg, for which Bryce was slightly jealous.

"They said that they'd been coming by here every couple of days since Mr. Krupps passed away." The officers were looking over the garage, and Noah was showing them what else they'd found. Devon continued when she nodded. "They

83

have an idea that he's doing this so that he can move in and find the money. Old man Krupp, he told everyone that he buried money on his land when he'd been a little boy."

"I see. What an idiot. Unless he did bury it." She looked at Devon when he didn't say anything. "You think he did. And that it really is out here on this land."

"I do. He came to me just after my sire died. Told me that he was concerned that someone was taking his money out of the bank. After a general search of the bank records, as well as some recordings that had been made, we found out that it was his daughter, Beth." She asked if he was serious. "I am, but she wasn't alone in her taking out the money. It looked as if Howard was making her do it. And in a couple of the recordings, it looks like he might have beaten her up a bit before going to the bank. Also, now we believe that he had a gun on her. So, when confronted, not only did she say that was right, but Beth divorced Howard and moved in with her father. That didn't set well with Howard, as Krupp would come to the door with a shotgun when he arrived. He didn't knock her around after that. But the money is buried here."

"I can find it." Devon said that he hoped that she could. "Do you have any idea how much it might be? I mean, will it be enough so that Beth can find herself someplace safe, and get Howard out of her life?"

"Oh, he'll be out of her life. That's a given. The police have enough evidence on him to know that he set the fire. What they don't know is how he did it. Noah is going to work on that for us." She looked at the expansiveness of the yard. "It wouldn't have been close to the house, if that helps.

That would be what Howard would think. Mr. Krupp wasn't crippled, but he didn't move very well."

Nodding, she walked into the back yard. Devon might think that it wasn't close to the house, but she had a feeling that it would have been, so that he could keep an eye on it. The man wasn't greedy, but he was smart. If he had figured out that someone was into his accounts, then he'd be smart in burying the money.

As soon as she was near the graveyard, she knew just where to look for the money. Bryce stood there near the little cemetery. It was cleaned up, just a little overgrown now that the mister was gone. The fresh grave there had no marker, but she wasn't concerned with that. He would have one, even if she had to get it for him herself. But the more she looked around, the more she realized how sad Mr. Krupps's life had been.

He and his wife had lost several children, all of them under the age of two. They were hard times then, and women didn't get the care that they did now. She read over each of the stones, her heart breaking for each little lamp that had been meticulously carved into the small stones. When she came to his wife, Elizabeth Krupp, she paused and read over the dates three times before it occurred to her what she was seeing. Turning when she heard a twig snap behind her, she looked at Noah.

"Beth isn't their child." She waited while Noah read over the headstones as well. "Beth was born four years after their last child died and took Elizabeth with her. There isn't any way that she's their child. What do you suppose happened?"

"I don't know. But I'm betting that we can find out." She nodded and took his hand into hers. "The police are going to wait inside and see if Howard comes by at some point. They're thinking he might be out trying to get himself a hotplate. That's the only thing he's missing to set up house here. What an idiot."

"Yes, I agree with you." She looked at the headstones again. "Noah, can we have children? I'm thinking not. But either way, I'd like to have us bring up some children together. All right? Even if we don't have them by our bodies, we can still have children, right?"

"No, we can't have children, you and I, but you're right. I'd love to bring children into our home and raise them. Also, if you'd not mind, I know that your mom and grandma are looking, but I'd very much like for them to stay with us. Unless they'd rather not. I mean, your grandmother, she does own this place, doesn't she?"

"They didn't want to intrude. And yes, she does own it—or she did. She signed it over to me when you moved in with me. I think she mentioned that it should be in the family again." He laughed when she did. "I'll talk to them. But it would go a long way in having them feel welcome if you told them that you'd like for them to stay as well."

He said that he would, and they headed home. She had some work to do. Finding out the real relationship between Beth and Mr. Krupp would be helpful. Bryce wondered if it would help solve a few things as well. Then tomorrow, she'd go and get the money.

Chapter 6

"If she decides to not disown her mother, then we challenge her. We'll be able to then sentence her to death. Or Bryce could choose to lose her magic. Either way, we come out winners. The very fact that we have to worry about this woman shows how our former leaders didn't do their job. She should never have gotten this strong." White nodded and Gray simply looked away. "Are you two even listening? I told you that if she wants, she could have us step down and then she'll take over running the WC. I can tell you right now, you won't have nearly the perks you have now from the Witches' Council."

"I thought when we had her father killed that would be the end of it. I mean, with a human mother, how were we to know that she'd become so strong? Not even her grandmother is as strong as any of us." Black knew that Bea had been teaching her granddaughter magic. But they'd never been able to catch

87

her at it. If they had, then she too would have been killed. "Perhaps we can make friends with her, show her that we're not as bad as she thinks we are."

"The moment that she gets to know us, she's going to know exactly what sort of people we are. From what I'm to understand about her, she needs only to touch us and she'll know all that we know, even things we might well have forgotten."

"Oh, that would be bad indeed." Black nodded. "Then she'll just have to be killed. I don't even like the idea that she could give up her magic. There could be repercussions with that as well. Yes, dead is better."

They had the most insidious names—Black, White, and Gray. He supposed it had to do with the fact that they were to see all sides, including the gray area of an issue that came up. All they'd ever been able to see, since realizing that they had all the power, was whatever gave them the most. They should have been called Green, he often thought. Green, as in they were getting all the perks and none of the bad shit that came along. They even had powers that they'd not had before. And Black had been his name for so long that he could no longer remember what he'd been called before.

"I have an idea." They all turned to White, the stupidest of all the witches that he knew. "Why don't we just tell her that we want her to behave herself? And to stay out of our business?"

"And what if that has just the opposite effect? That she just decides that, since we want her to stay out of our business, she'll dig deeper? What do you think she'll do when she finds out that we've imprisoned several witches for no other reason than we could? That we have parties nightly with humans, then kill them? Do you think she'll just turn a blind eye to that?"

"No. She'd probably be mad."

Black rolled his eyes at the man. Christ, did they have to put a brilliant man like himself together with two of the most ignorant warlocks on the planet? He supposed that was what they meant when they said it was a balance. To him it was just annoying.

"We need a plan. One that will make us look good and for her to no longer be a threat to us. I'm willing to listen to any and all *good* ideas. No more stupid ones about asking her to be friends with us." White shook his head. He didn't say much, but when he did, you had to stare at him for several seconds to realize that whatever had spewed from his mouth had really been what he'd said. "This plan has to be smart too. And even though I doubt very much that either of you can come up with one that is, we still need to work together on this."

"I don't remember. Who is it that put you in charge?" Black wanted to get up and smack the shit out of Gray, but he'd tried that before and couldn't use his hand for a month. "Why don't we try and deal with this? The last time you dealt with someone, we had the Wolf Council, as well as the Vampire League, on our asses."

"I've told you several times, I had no idea that woman was a half breed. When we were allotted this position, they took away our ability to tell what other creatures are, except witches. And since you can't tell either, how the hell were any of us to know?" Gray told him that he could have simply left the woman alone. "And given up on the best night of sex I've ever had? I don't think so. And if I remember correctly, you came about six times yourself that night. So, don't go all sanctimonious on me now."

Neither of them said anything, nor did they have any suggestions. So, once again, he'd have to plan it all out and make sure that it was done right. Damn it all to fuck and back, where was a nosey neighbor when you needed one?

Of course, there hadn't been one in the first place with Austin. He'd been in the back yard, teaching his little girl how to use her powers. Black had seen them together, and before he realized how strong Bryce was, he hated the fact that the two of them were having such a good time. And they seemed to genuinely love each other. What really pissed him off was the human mother just sitting there observing their magic, more than likely ready to learn it herself—not that she could. He'd ever allow that. It was as if she, as a human being, had some right to be watching them.

After the other two had annoyed him to no end, he left them to whatever they did when he wasn't around. More than likely they just sat around, not speaking, not even blinking until he said their names. He was working with idiots; plain and simple, they were idiots.

Black had never liked Austin. None of the other warlocks really, but he'd despised Austin. Black only had his job because Austin had turned it down. He'd wanted to spend more time with his growing family. Like anyone wanted to hang out with a child and a human. But apparently there was no accounting for taste in some.

Austin had been strong too, stronger than any other warlock that Black had ever met. And that had terrified him. The thought of him deciding that he'd had enough of his family and wanted to have the seat that Black had taken made him plot and plan like he'd never done before. And it had worked — to a point.

Black had planned to take his mother too. Bea — what a ridiculous name for someone — had been watching Black like a hawk since before her son had made his decision. And Black was reasonably sure that she knew a great deal more about him and the other two than they wanted her to know. Like the fact that they were killing witches because they might someday be stronger than them.

Killing a witch for power was fine, but they had to be stronger than you. And that was a biggie. But they also would have had to have done something to you to warrant such behavior, such as slighting you in some way. Or — and this one was what he'd been using — they had to do something that the WC had deemed bad for their kind.

Not in the last hundred or so years had a single witch who they'd — mostly him — deemed bad for their kind done anything more than be in Black's way when he'd wanted something. And Black thought that there could never be anything that he didn't want.

Making his way to his private rooms, he opened the lock and walked in. He had so much in his one room alone that he knew that it would get him killed. There were magic books; all witches had them, and he'd taken as many of them as he could. He had brooms and hats. Most of them were decorative, but he'd taken them because he could. Black had bits and pieces of magical spells, seeds for herbs that no one else had. He'd even taken clips of hair, knowing that magic, very strong magic, could read them and find out all sorts of things about the person who'd had them. Magic; it was all here, and the saddest part was he couldn't use it, nor could he glean what was in the books because of what he was.

When they'd been given their positions, the best part of him had been taken away. None of them could do a great many things that would have made them stronger. Not only could they not see what a person was—that was small in comparison to some of the things they couldn't do—but they couldn't read other magical books. Couldn't gain more magic from killing a witch or warlock. And when they stepped down, their power, the power that they'd gotten for being on the WC, would be taken from them and they'd have to start from scratch.

That was why he'd been collecting over the years—to be able to have all this to build himself up with again and do it quickly. But that wouldn't mean shit if Bryce was out there too. She'd take him down so quickly that he'd never have a chance to fight back.

"Fucking witch should never have been allowed to be conceived." Black just didn't understand it. Why did the council allow a half-breed child to become a part of the world that he had come to love? "Magic is everything."

And it was too—in everything; a part of everything.

92

Everything was even made by magic as far as he was concerned. Touching the book that he'd taken from Austin, he wondered what the family would say if they knew that he had it. They'd more than likely kill him. That was precisely why it was in here and not out in his home where he could brag about it.

"Someday I'll lay it next to his mother and daughter's books." He thought of the stand that he'd had made especially for the three of them to be side by side. "Yes, that'll be a day that will make me a god to all the witches. Not only will I have their books, but I will have their power too."

Giggling, something that he only did in private, he even did a little dance to go with it. Soon, he kept telling himself. Soon it would be over for the Frost family, and he'd be able to make the rules, ones that would cut out the half-breeds altogether.

Black was just leaving his treasure trove when he felt the tingle of being summoned. If those idiots were calling him to have him tell them how to breathe, he was going to remove their heads once and for all. Going to the room that was reserved only for those he deemed necessary, Black felt his cock shrivel up and nearly make its way up his ass. His adversary was standing there as if she owned the place.

"Hello, Black." He asked her what she wanted, and when she smiled at him, he sat down in his seat so that she'd not be able to see his knees shaking. "I have a request. Not that I really care if you grant it or not. Should I want to, I'm sure that I could make you wish you'd never been born."

"You think? I do not. What is it that I can turn down

93

for you today, Bryce Frost? Are you asking to take a mate? Then I say nay. Are you telling me that you've had enough of your mother? Then I would grant that one. Ask me. I have a great many things to do today." She laughed and told him that she'd never do either one. Black wasn't sure what she'd meant with her answer. "Tell me what it is you think you need. I am a very busy man, and I don't have time for your childish games."

"I wish for you to release the hold you have on a human family." He asked her what she meant. "There has been a murder, and I want—"

"I have killed no one." She said that he lied, and she'd never said that he had. "Then what is it you think I have over a family? I'm assuming that they're human?"

"Yes. But that's not what I'm asking for. As I was saying, there has been a murder, and to solve it, I will need their files and all the families that are attached to it. The name is Carter."

"I know no such name. So, it stands to reason that I would have no hold over them." She asked him if he'd release it to her. "Yes, whatever it takes to get you out of my offices. As I have said, I'm very busy. Now, if there is nothing else, then I'd like for you to leave."

"I want my father's things." His balls and cock, already the size of a peanut from earlier with her, seemed to have leapt from his body and into his ass. Shifting on the chair to try and get some relief from the pain of it, he realized she was still speaking.

"Why is it you think you have a need for those?"

"Well, he was my father. And since the council had him

94

murdered, then his things would rightfully come to me, as his daughter and a witch of worth." He laughed. It was better than what he felt he needed to do, and that was to puke then run for his room. "Did you hear a word that I said? I want his things. And along with it, his books. You've no use for them, and I'd like them returned to me. As they should have been years ago. I am well within my rights to ask for them and to have them returned."

"You are. I'm going to see about having that law taken off the books too. Why should you have his things when he was killed, not murdered, for something that he did wrong?" She asked him what that had been. "He broke the laws of our kind, and you well know it. Had you not been greedy and had him train you, nothing more than a half-breed animal—"

His airway was cut off. Black could feel the tightness around his heart and lungs. Spots before his eyes made Bryce go in and out of focus. When his hands began to tingle, all he could think about was that all his planning had been for naught. Bryce was stronger than anyone he knew, much stronger.

He realized that she was speaking, saying something about his welfare, asking if he was all right. The smile she gave him was as big as her face—evil looking, he thought, like she was some sort of monster that was going to eat him alive. Then he was free.

Gathering as much wind into his lungs as he could hurt. The burning of his throat hurt him with each swallow. Coughing, he saw a spot of blood on his desk in front of where he'd been sitting. Black looked at Bryce when she asked him, once again, if he was all right.

"You're going to pay for this." She said that she thought that it could be wiped up with a tissue. The blood wasn't that big a deal. "Not that, you moronic fuck. I'm talking about attacking me. You cannot touch me, I am the council. I'll make you pay if it's the last thing—"

"It just might be." The threat—and there wasn't any doubt that's what it was—hung there between them like a pink elephant in a dark forest. "Now, as I was requesting—and so you know, this is not so much a request as it is a demand—I want my father's things back by the end of the week. And that would include his magic book. If I don't have them, Black.... Well, trust me, you don't want to know what I'll do to you if I have to get them for myself."

Then she was gone. But her laughter, high and full of humor, lingered in the room like a woman's perfume. The sound of it—again, much like a perfume that a woman would spritz on to entice a man—made the air around him tight. But unlike the smell, there was a clogging of his throat, and his ears were full of the sounds. Black knew that as surely as he sat here, he was going to die by her hand if he did not do something, and soon. Bryce wasn't one to fuck with anymore.

~*~

Noah waited for Bryce to come out of the bathroom. She'd been in there since returning this afternoon, about an hour ago, and each time he'd knocked on the door to find out if she was all right, she told him to go away. Actually, she wasn't quite that nice about it, but he'd gotten the point. When Laura came into the hallway where he was, she asked him what was

96

going on.

"She went to see about some file that she needed from the WC. And to ask for her father's books. She said that it had been long enough." Laura nodded, but looked so pained that he changed the subject. "This file, she said that it has a hold on it from one of the members. Black. Then, of course, she had to explain to me that there were three men of the WC — Black, White, and Gray."

"Yes, there are. Black is the meanest of the three of them. White — well, Austin often said that he was the calming one, but he was also very vain about things. Gray, I was told, was stupid. And his gray matter wasn't much more than a tater tot with ketchup on it." They both laughed, and just then, Bryce came out of the bathroom. She looked a little green. "So, you tangled with Black, did you? You should have taken me with you. I would love to have seen his face when a non-witch came in the room with you."

"He killed Father." Bryce staggered to the living room after saying that. Both he and Laura made their way behind her as Bea was joining them. "He killed my father for no other reason than he wanted me to fail. I mean, he had no idea how powerful I was then, and regrets not killing me too. But he killed my dad. There hadn't been any complaints about us either."

They sat down, Noah next to Bryce. And when she wrapped herself around him, she was chilled and shivering. When he wrapped his arms around her, she cuddled under his chin while she continued to tell them what she'd encountered.

"I asked first for the file. But something came to me while

I was there that made me think that I had to ask for it under the name Carter, not Krupp. Once he gave me permission to open the file, I reached into his mind and saw what he'd done to my father. Done for no other reason than he could." Bea asked why he had targeted Austin. "Because he could see him training me off and on. Saw us in the back yard playing around, and he was jealous. And when it occurred to him what he was — the law, so to speak — he came up with the plan to have someone complain, then to kill him."

No one said anything for several minutes. They were thinking, he could see that. But he also knew that the man who was called Black would not be long for this world if he thought that he could get away with what he'd done. Noah asked about the file and what the significance was with the names.

"He knows the girl — Beth Krupp Carter. Well, he doesn't know her, not at all, but he's related to her. She's his daughter." Noah asked her what she'd said, and Laura started laughing. "Yeah, he's got himself a half-breed daughter of his own. So all the rules that he's been trying to tell us about people like my mom, they're not going to mean squat because he has done it all himself."

"I don't understand." Bryce explained it to him. "Christ, he's taken a human to his bed and she had a child by him? Holy shit, Bryce. This isn't just about the rules he's trying to enforce over your mom. His kind — the council — cannot have any children. Not ever."

"Why not? I mean, even the thought of him reproducing makes me ill, but I don't understand the reasoning behind

98

them not having anyone to love them." Before Noah could explain, Laura seemed to have gotten it. "So, they cannot be used against them. Oh my, I never thought of that until just this second. The council wouldn't want someone to have the upper hand over them by taking their children. And I bet that it's happened before, so that's the reason for the rule."

"Exactly. And the fact that he had a child makes him subject to all sorts of fines and sentencing." Noah let Bryce slide to the couch. She was looking better all the time. "What did he do to you that I'm going to have to kill him for?"

"Nothing. Just taking a walk into his mind was enough." She shivered again and got up to move around the room. "I've asked for — well, demanded really — my father's things back. He has them. I've even seen the room that he has it all stored in, the code to get into the room, and his plans for using it when he's either asked to step down or he changes the rules. He thinks that will be done once I'm dead. Also, he has it out for you, Grandma."

"Good. I'd hate to have to kill the little bastard and not have just cause." Everyone turned and looked at her. It was the first time he'd ever heard her curse. "What? I've been around the block a time or two, you know. You don't get to be my age and have a son and not hear a few things you store away for later. Why, I bet I could teach you a thing or two about sex."

Everyone yelled "Don't" at the same time. Grandma, as he'd been asked to call her, laughed. He thought about living out the rest of their lives together and thought there would never be a time when he was bored.

They talked for another hour. Mostly it was about the things that they'd do with Black if he didn't turn over the things that were Bryce's father's. Noah didn't have any idea what they might be; a book that had spells in it was the only thing that he really understood. But he didn't care really — whatever it was, he wanted Bryce to have it.

When his cell phone rang, he went out onto the deck to answer it. There were some very heated discussions going on about the coming fall soloistic. Again, he didn't know what that meant, but he was willing to do whatever it took to make his love happy.

"There are a couple of things that I'd like to talk over... where are you?" He told his old boss, Lin Ming, where he currently was. "The United Kingdom? What on earth is there that you had to travel halfway around the world for?"

"My bride." That shut the other man up. "I came here to see to a few things and get some vacation time in when I met her. She's wonderful, and I couldn't be happier. And before you ask, no, I'm not returning to live in the States anytime soon."

"But I thought we had a deal. You'd work for me until you keeled over in your grave, and I'd be able to retire with a clean slate." That wasn't going to happen either, but Noah laughed when he did. "Seriously though, congratulations. I'm very happy for you both. But I have to ask, is she blind? I mean, she'd have to be if she wanted to stay with your ugly puss."

They talked about nothing at all for several minutes, and Noah could tell that he was building up to something.

Coming into the house, he sat at the desk that he'd claimed for his own. And when he finally hit on it, Noah sat down to think about what was going on. He also found out that not only had Boseman been fired, but what was left of his crew was gone as well.

"I have a case that I'd like you to give some thought on. I know you're far away, but I can send you what I have, and I think you can see what I'm not." He asked him what the case was about. "Murder. What else is there in this town? Anyway, the man is claiming that he shot his wife in self-defense. I say he shot her because of an argument that they'd been having over the last few days. Something about a lover. I was never sure if it was his lover or hers, but I'll send it all to you. If you have a fax machine or a computer nearby, I can tell you what you'll be looking at."

"I think there is one here. Let me call you right back when I get it figured out." Lin thanked him. "Anytime, I told you that."

William flew into the room seconds after Noah hung up. After telling the faerie what he needed, he said that he'd see if his mistress had one. Noah needed to get him a faerie. They'd been sharing William, but he still needed to find one of his own. When William came back, saying that his mistress had made him one, the machine appeared on the corner of the desk. After calling Lin back, he was getting the paperwork in minutes.

"The page that you have first is of the crime scene. As you can see, she was shot in the heart. If she had one, my guy is saying, but they were having a fight when she pulled out the gun first. When she shot at him, the report knocked the gun out of her hand and he picked it up. She then threw a knife at him and he shot to kill." He asked him if he had a picture of the knife in the wall. "I do. A close up, as a matter of fact. But I don't think I'd be bringing a knife to a gun fight, do you?"

The picture of the knife came through the machine last. He looked at it, then smiled. It was about as cut and dried as he'd ever seen. Just as he was leaning back in the chair, Bryce came in the room with an envelope.

"He killed her, but not in self-defense. The knife was planted after he killed her." Lin asked how he could tell. "From where she is lying on the floor. I'm assuming that it's about fifteen to twenty feet from her to the wall. There isn't any way that that sort of knife, a butter knife, would have been planted that deeply by her tossing it, unless that's what she did for a living. But regardless, it's a butter knife. Your guy planted it after he killed his wife."

After he hung up, Bryce sat on his lap, her legs on either side of his hips. Noah felt his cock harden at the thought of taking her right where she was. Asking her where her family was, she said that she'd sent them away for the morning. Noah tore off her shirt even before she finished the sentence.

Chapter 7

Bryce couldn't seem to get enough of her mate. He only needed to touch her, to come close enough for her to touch him and she'd be wet, her body ready for him. And right now, sitting on his lap, his mouth doing amazing things to her breasts, she began rubbing her hands on his thick hard cock.

"You're making me insane — you know that, don't you?" Bryce told Noah that she thought he was already there. "Yes, well, it's all your fault. Before you came into my life, I was a smart, reasonable man. Now I'm nothing more than a pile of mushy love for my mate."

She was naked before him, and she took the opportunity to spread herself out over his desk. There were a few things that bit into her back, but when he stood up, as naked as her, his cock in his hand, she didn't care if her hand was in a bear trap — she wanted him.

"Christ, seeing you here like this, all I can think about is feasting on you. But I need to be inside of you too. Marry me, Bryce." She told him no and spread her legs wider, sliding her hand down to her pussy until she could feel the heat coming from it. "Touch yourself, Bryce. Let me see you bring yourself."

She only needed to touch her fingers to her clit to come, but she played around it, gathering her juices on her fingers before she took her hand to his mouth. When Noah suckled them beyond his lips, using her other hand, she touched her clit and screamed how hard she was coming.

As her second climax took her under, she screamed out his name, telling him to take her, begging for his cock. But he was teasing her now, using the tip of his cock to bring her over and over while he suckled at her breasts.

Bryce was on fire now, her body burning not just to feel him inside of her, but to feel his cum filling her. The heat of his release would bring her over, she knew that, but it would be epic; her own release would take her under. When he slammed into her, filling her to the hilt with his cock, Bryce screamed again and again, her throat raw from it as he pounded her hard enough to move the desk several inches from where it had been.

When he came, his body bowing back from hers, she felt the pause—like every living thing, every air molecule in the world, just waited to see how Noah would react, how his body would let go. And when he did, she felt the impact of the explosion all through her body.

Bryce screamed. It came from her mind, her body—even her heart seemed to want to let the world know that they'd been a part of something spectacular. Something so profound that worlds colliding couldn't have been nearly as epic.

But Noah wasn't finished. Jerking her up from the desk, he bent her over it, her ass so near his thickening cock that she could feel the heat from it. And when he leaned over her, his cock pounding her from behind, he told her to come for him.

His voice was harsh, raspy, like he was having a hard time holding onto his beast. And when his nails, claws really, dug deeply into her back along her spine, she tensed up for whatever he was giving her. When he told her to come again, again, with the raw voice that she didn't recognize, she came hard, her body obeying his command like she was his.

The teeth that sank into her ribcage took her breath away. They weren't his, not Noah's the human. And when they tore viciously at her flesh, breaking bones and splitting her open, Bryce screamed again, the pain so severe that she knew she was going to die.

It took her several seconds to realize that Noah was speaking to her. His voice this time was frantic with worry. He was holding her in his arms, and they were seated on the couch in his office. Looking up at him, she saw him burst into tears and Bryce wiped them away with her finger.

"I thought that we'd killed you." She started to tell him that she'd thought that as well but didn't get the chance. "I don't know what happened. I mean, I do know—I just don't understand why that happened. I have never in all my life—"

She put her fingers over his mouth. "Too many words. Slow down." He smiled around her fingers. "I don't know what that was either, but I'm not sore. Am I bleeding or

105

anything?"

"No. You were, but not now. It just sort of healed up on its own. Christ, I will never do that to you again." She sat up slowly; truthfully, she was almost too afraid to see if she was going to be in pain. "You're going to be all right, aren't you? I have never been so terrified in all my life. I'm so sorry."

"I'm not. That was fantastic, Noah. And while I don't think I'd like to have sex like that every time, I'd love for you to lose control on occasion." Stretching, she turned to look at him before something occurred to her. "Your dragon—he bit me, didn't he?"

"Yes. Well, sort of, I guess. That's what frightened me so badly. He sort of took me over in ways so that he could bite you. And when he tore into your flesh, I thought for sure that he was trying to murder you." She nodded. "Are you mad?"

"Good heavens no. As I said, it was amazing sex, but not for daily use. I suppose it was his way of marking me or making me his own. I'm all right with that." She smiled at him. "You solved a case over the phone. But I have a feeling that it was much more than just a knife being planted in the wall. When I heard you say that, I wondered why the man hadn't used something sharper, something...I don't know, like another gun or something."

"He might have. But as soon as I touched the photograph with the knife in it, it was like my mind centered on it and I could actually see him planting the knife." Noah handed her the other picture, the one where the wife was on the floor. "Tell me what you feel when you touch this one."

The actions of the man came flooding at her when she

touched the picture of the body. The wife was coming in the kitchen to ask him where the house payment money was, and he shot her in the chest. There wasn't a row, as he'd said, but just him killing her. And as soon as he heard the sirens, he panicked, grabbed the first knife he could find, and rammed it into the wall. Bryce looked at Noah.

"That's fucking freaky." He said it had been for him too, but he'd been almost afraid to say anything. "Yeah, I can understand that. So, you think that we'll have this...whatever this is all the time? Or was this a one timer?"

He handed her another picture in a frame. Bryce backed from it and Noah laughed. She was just fine thinking that it was a one-time thing. And if they had to use it again, then she'd deal with it then. Right now, she was feeling too good to think about it.

The rest of the afternoon was spent on different projects. Bryce had several things going at one time, one of which was trying to work out a way to get the WC replaced. When she'd been there the other day, she realized that all of them were corrupt. But the issue she was having, among other things, was who did she talk to about getting them investigated? And after that, who did they get to replace them?

She knew that Black had it in his head that she was going to take the job from him. But she didn't want it. There were too many things in her life that she wanted to explore, to test. And if she was forever settling one spat, or rule broken, after another, she'd never get to spend as much time with Noah as she wanted. Bryce thought that they'd make a good team to do some investigative work for different areas of insurance, as well as for the police.

Mom came to see her just before supper. She said that she had a few questions that she needed to get answered and wanted her to go with her into town. Bryce could see that whatever it was, Mom was really upset about it.

As they were making their way through the light traffic, Bryce asked her what it was. For a few minutes, she didn't think her mom was going to answer her. But when she turned to her with tears in her eyes, Bryce felt something in her heart stir for her.

"I was just taking a walk yesterday and heard a child crying. It was in the back yard of one of those row houses— you know the kind. Where they are federally subsidized. and most of the people there have one thing or another that prevents them from working." Bryce told her that not all but a few, she thought. "Yes, well, I was trying my best to be kind. And politically correct. Anyway, I went to see what all the crying was about. And there in the back yard was a little child chained up to a dog house. Like a dog. Bryce, it was all I could do not to go there and steal that child away."

"You didn't, did you, Mom?" She said that she hadn't yet. "Good. And if it comes to that, let me do it. I have more magic than you and can zap the ass of anyone that is fucking with a child."

"Such language. What if the child were yours and that was its first word?" Bryce only smiled at her mom. "I see. Well, it's a good thing that I'm living with you so that I can be a saving grace for the child. Back to this child. No, I didn't steal it away, but I did watch him. He couldn't have been any more than about five or so. And he saw me looking."

She waited on her mom to tell her the rest. And when they pulled up in front of the row houses, Bryce reached out with this freaky power and knew which house it was. She reached out to Lady Kelly, to ask her for her help. It was, after all, her township.

The Baldwin home. Yes, I know of it. I'd not heard that they had any children, however. I'll meet you there, unless you want to go ahead and do your witchy stuff on them and save that little mite. By the way, I've heard that you're helping out with cases across the pond, as they call it here. You might want to talk to the constable here. I think he has a few unsolved as well. She told Kelly that she thought that Noah was already helping him. *Good. I think the man is set to retire soon. Maybe one of you guys could put in for the job. Lord knows that we need someone on the staff that isn't nine hundred years old.*

I'm sure that Noah is already older than that. They both laughed. *I'll talk to him about it. I know that we're both finding our way around here. I have some things I'm doing right now for the WC, sort of a covert kind of thing.*

If you need our help, let me know. I think that the faerie queen has been having some issues with them too. Something about her having to send faeries to them once a month to clean their offices and homes. Why would they have to do that? She said she didn't think that was right either but would add it to her list. *I'll tell her. And set up a meeting with her. I'm sure you know more rules about that office than she or I would ever know.*

When Kelly showed up at the place where they were parked, Bryce's mom told Kelly what was going on. She told her, too, about how the child had been out there during the cold night. She'd come to check on him at about midnight and had left him a sandwich.

"I just couldn't see him starving because his parents need to be killed." Bryce looked at her mother, shocked at her lately. "Well, the only thing I can think of is that you and your grandma are rubbing off on me. I feel better than I have in years."

Knocking on the door, they waited for someone to come to it. There was shouting going on inside. They could even hear someone sobbing. Just as she was ready to open the door on her own, a woman opened it, and Bryce knew this wasn't going to go well.

~*~

The fire was being contained, mostly due to Bryce. When Noah had arrived on the scene, he'd been completely blown away by the state of the fire. He'd been told that it had only been burning for several minutes when he'd been called there. But nearly every bit of the home and the contents were ash. He looked over at the body that was covered with a gray tarp. When Laura came to him, he took her into his arms. She was devastated about the entire thing, he'd surmised.

"They took them all three to the hospital. What kind of person does that to their own family?" He said that it was more common than not. "I don't know if you are aware of this or not, but when a woman is venting, they don't need you to make it worse by commenting."

"Sorry." He had to hide a smile. Laura had just scolded him with a grin on her face, much like his own mother would have done. "Anyway, as you were saying about people and their families."

"Yes. He had beaten the woman only a few minutes before we arrived. To think we were just sitting there in the car, waiting, when we could have kept her from being hurt so badly." He asked if she was going to make it. "Yes. Because of Kelly. She did something — I'm not sure what — to her and she was healed. I think that Bryce could have done it, but she was much too busy keeping the other homes from burning to the ground. I had no idea that Kelly was a dragon as well."

"Yes. When Devon married her, she was looking through the portraits on the walls when his mother's dragon came to live inside of Kelly. I've never seen it happen — I guess it's very rare. They're very happy, and her dragon and Kelly have been getting used to each other." She asked him if that would happen to Bryce. "I don't know. All the paintings of my family were sold off when my family got behind in the taxes. I guess they had no idea that they weren't being paid by their solicitor."

"I'm so sorry to hear that, Noah. This makes it better, I think, that you not only got your home back, but you also gained a mate. I'm assuming that you're going to be marrying my daughter soon, correct?" He laughed. Noah just couldn't help it. Hugging her to him, he assured her that all he had to do was convince Bryce that it was a good idea. "I'll work on her. Guilt her, actually. Can't have my favorite son-in-law not married, now can we?"

"No, ma'am, we cannot."

Noah watched the firemen walk around the site. The

house was completely gone—not even a stick of furniture could be seen in the rubble. The woman and her children were going to need help.

Devon asked him if he had a minute. Leaving Laura, Noah walked to the other side of the street.

"I have two homes that they can move into. The issue is, there is very little in the way of furniture. Not to mention, clothing is needed for all three of them. The little boy, he'll need to be in the hospital for a few days. He's dehydrated, as well as malnourished. They all are, but he is by far the worse of the three of them." Devon looked over at the body and continued. "Kelly said that he came out the door with a gun after the missus was pulled out. Had she not had the child in her arms and the other one locked in the yard, she told me she didn't know what might have happened."

"We have Laura to thank for saving them," Noah told Devon. "She had seen the little boy out back yesterday and brought Bryce here. And since she didn't want to step on any toes, Bryce called in Kelly. I'm glad that they were all here to help. I did tell them, and I hope you don't mind, that if anything like this happened again, to take care of it. Not to wait on anyone." Devon told him that was good. He didn't want anyone hurt, however. "Not unless it's the bad guy, I'm assuming."

Devon was nodding as he spoke again. "Yes, well, I'm glad that piece of shit is taken care of too. Had I been here and he pulled out a gun on them, I don't think the block would have survived." Devon said that he would have been lucky if the entire town had survived. "But they did well. And Bryce said that Kelly was so calm the entire time. Then she fell apart."

"She told me that she hated to kill anyone, but he'd nearly killed his wife." The husband had killed his wife, from what Noah had heard from Bryce, but he said nothing as Devon spoke.

"As I was saying earlier, they're going to need a great many things. I'm going into town to see what I can find. And I was wondering if you'd like to come along."

Noah thanked him and thought of something. "Sure. But only if you let me pay for half of it." Devon said that he was counting on that. "They'll need food too. How about we send some of our staff to do that? And Bryce and Kelly can go get clothing for them all."

"Fantastic. All right. We're organized, so let's get to it." Devon told him he'd drive, and they made their way to the car. Then he stopped and turned to him. "I suppose we should tell the women before we just leave them."

After talking to the women and getting their cooks involved, they were off to get whatever they might need.

The house that Devon had was a four bedroom with a nice big yard. They were close to the library, as well as walking distance to the local school. Noah was trying to think about a job for the woman and realized that he'd not heard any of their names. He asked Bryce what she knew.

The mothers name is Bobbie Fredrick — short for Roberta. The older boy is Josh, and the baby is Blake. Josh is seven; very small for his age, but we're going to be working on that. And Blake needs to eat better, as do the rest, and be able to get out and move. He's about nine months old, Bobbie told me. I'm at the hospital now. He asked her if she could find out sizes for them. *Sure. Kelly has already come in and gotten all that, including shoe sizes. I guess you guys are taking care of the household items.*

Yes. I have never had to shop before. And neither has Devon. Things in both our homes were there when we were children. I know that he's gotten a few things with Kelly, but she's done most of that sort of thing. Devon called in his mother to help. She's been tisking at him since he asked her. They both laughed, and then he felt her tension. *What is it, love? Something I need to come there about?*

The WC is here. I'm not worried about them, but they're here. I don't think it's because of me, however. He waited when she asked him to. After telling Devon, the other dragon asked if they needed to go there. Telling him to wait was about the hardest thing he'd done. *They're not here for me. One of them is here watching over a woman. I'm going to see what I can find out. I'll be careful.*

He told Devon but was worried. Devon said that she was with Kelly and should be fine. If not, they'd both have to add an entire new wing of the hospital, as well as a burn unit. Noah told him that he wasn't the least bit funny. He was still laughing when they met up with Devon's mom at the furniture store. Noah decided that he was going to think of some way of getting back at him.

The shopping was a great deal more fun than he'd thought it would be. Not only did they get everything that Lady Susanna told them, but a few extras for the children. He had so much fun in that department that the conversation that he and Bryce had had about children made him want to

114

hurry out and get one for themselves. Lady Susanna came to help him with the blankets he was picking out.

"I have so many things that belonged to my daughter, and then to Devon. I thought that my heart would shatter when she passed away. After losing the first child by that bastard she was married to, I should have brought her home. It wasn't his child, and even though he knew that when they wed, he still threw her down the stairs not long after they were married to abort the babe. Then she got pregnant with his child—Devon was that baby." She looked to where Devon was and watched him testing out strollers. "If I had, however, I'd never have had him. And he almost makes up for having to put up with his father for all those years."

"He killed him, didn't he?" It wasn't an easy question, but he really wanted to know. "There is talk that Devon knocked him down the stairs as his dragon. Not one person that mentions it to me says anything terrible about Devon. They actually seem very proud of him. But they know that it wasn't an accident."

"When I came to see him after the funeral, he told me that I could live here. My first question to him was what he was going to demand of me." She looked at him now. "He told me that he wanted nothing and thought that I was a grown woman and could decide things on my own. So, I have. And being with him, and now Kelly, has made life worth living again. Also, being a great-grandmother isn't all that shabby either."

"Yes, I can see that you're very heartbroken about the prospect of being one." She smiled at him, and he could

115

almost feel the love of it all the way to his own heart. "I have a favor to ask of you, Lady Susanna. I want to marry Bryce, and as I've only asked her the one time and she turned me down, I think that I'm going to get the same answer again—if she lets me ask. Every time I start to, she covers my mouth. It's a good distraction, but it's not getting us wed."

"Yes, I can well imagine that she's very good at distracting all manner of things when she has it in her mind not to talk about something. I've asked her several hundred times a day to stop calling me Lady Susanna, much as I have you, and neither of you have done it. I will stop answering the two of you if you don't just call me Susanna." She eyed him like he was a bug on a glass slide under a microscope. "Well?"

"Susanna, you are beautiful, and I would appreciate it if you helped me with my future wife." Susanna said well done. "Yes. I don't think you gave me much of a choice, but I do love you dearly."

Arranging to have everything delivered was smart, because as they were checking out, it occurred to both him and Devon how much furniture it took to fill a house that size. But the people were very polite and nice. They were even going to set it up for them when they got to the house. Christ, he'd not thought of that either.

He was still waiting to hear from Bryce when they were headed to their truck. She said she was fine but had some great news. Unless she had killed that guy, he couldn't think of a single thing that was good about the WC. As soon as they were at the house, he forgot about everything but the things they had to do yet.

By the time they were finished, and everything was where it was supposed to be, he was ready for his own home. But the house was ready for the family. Susanna had even hired them a small staff so that they could continue to mend and get stronger. The children needed their mother to be well, not trying to heal and take care of them at the same time. Noah thought it was an excellent idea. But he, too, was exhausted, and since Bryce had beaten him to bed, he nearly fell in it beside her without taking off his clothing.

Tomorrow he had a lot to do, and he still had to talk to Bryce about the WC at the hospital. Things, he had a feeling, were about to get bad. And he was sort of looking forward to it.

Chapter 8

Gray thought about the conversation that he'd had with the grand witch. He knew that she was in the area where he was. And he also knew that she was a great deal stronger than anyone, including Black, thought she was.

As soon as she'd come into the room, he stood up and bowed low to her. When she gave him permission to stand, he sat on the floor. He had been taught all the rules governing witches, and when one was as strong as Bryce, he had to never let his head be above her heart.

"You know what happened to this woman? Someone raped her so badly that she may well have died had you not brought her here." He said that he knew, and who had done it. "It was Black, wasn't it? He hurt her."

"Yes, mistress. He has hurt many more, but I never found them until it was much too late to save them." Gray looked over at the dying woman. "I fear that I didn't find her in time."

Bryce touched her fingers to the woman's head, and he watched in awe as the readings from the heart monitor, as well as the other machines on her, seemed to get stronger. He could hear her heart beating better as well. When Bryce sat down, he thanked her.

"There is no reason to thank me for saving someone that shouldn't have been made to hurt in the first place. You do, however, know what this means with the WC, don't you?" He nodded and smiled at her. "You knew this was going to happen before coming here with her."

"I had hoped it would. I had no way of knowing that you'd be here, but if you had not shown up, I was going to find you and throw myself at your mercy. Not that I deserve it. But I would wish that you'd let me tell you all before you behead me." She nodded, and while he was relieved to be able to clear his heart and mind, he really didn't want to die. "Black has been raping and murdering women for many years. Decades, I believe. I have lost track of time over the years, and I cannot tell you for how long. But nearly from the beginning." She asked him about children. "He has three that I am aware of. I have hidden away two of them. The third one he wishes to just take his chances with, he told me. I thought him to not care. He has so very little in life."

"I would like their names." Gray told her that he had a file on each of them that he would make sure that she got. "What about the women? Why does he not just have sex with them then let them go?"

"I think he believes that he is above all laws. He has it in his head that I'm stupid. It is a belief that I have played up for him. I have a great many things that I have stashed away, all of which I will give to you. In the event that I would have been killed before I stepped down, which I was planning to do soon anyway, they were to be hand delivered to you. Pictures, names, and places that I know that he has buried the dead." Bryce nodded and asked him to go on. "He wishes you dead, and thinks that by taking your mother, or now your mate, he can control you in your grief. I think he is under the assumption that you will be so grief stricken that you will simply let him kill you. I have a feeling that you are not so easily dissuaded."

"I am not. Is it true that you cannot tell what other creatures are? That you can only know that a shifter is a shifter when told?" He nodded, and wanted to ask her why she'd asked, but didn't. And she didn't elaborate. "Is White involved in any of this?"

"No, mistress. He *is* stupid." She laughed, and he wondered at that, but again, didn't ask. She was listening to him, and that was more than he could have hoped for. "The list of names isn't all the women, nor the dead. I didn't find out about it in time to make sure that there was an accounting for them. And if you were to ask me why I didn't turn him in before now, it is because there wasn't a witch strong enough to have taken him on until you."

"Why?" He asked her what she meant. "Why is it you think that I'm so strong? I'm no different than any other witch that I know. Even my grandmother can do a great many things—not only better, but there is just more that she can do."

121

He asked for permission to stand up and to touch her. When she nodded, he stood and could feel his knees shaking, and his hands were just as bad as he reached out to lay just a finger onto her shoulder. Gray closed his eyes, thinking of the pain he was going to be in when he showed her what she could do. Bryce asked him to tell her what he was doing.

"I am a lesser witch. I have powers, yes, given to me by becoming what I am. But you are so much more powerful that should I only touch you, as a lesser, then your power will show me what you are. And you." She asked again what would happen. Instead of answering her, he simply put his hand on her shoulder.

The pain of it radiated up his arm and to his head. As soon as the pain took his breath away, he was tossed across the room, where he hit the wall. Bones broke—he knew that even before she helped him to rise, and in turn, healed him. Gray also knew that she had every bit of information that she'd ever need from him concerning his life, that of the men he worked with, and how he felt about them both.

"The next time someone asks you what is going to happen when you do something like that, tell them. You nearly gave me a heart attack. Of all the stupid things to do." He was healed by the time she sat him on the chair that she'd been in. When he started to slide to the floor, she glared at him. "You sit on the floor again, and I will do something more than what you just did to yourself; you understand me?"

"Yes, mistress." He had to fight hard to hide a smile. She was going to be able to take care of the WC and run it better than anyone had before. "Black's plans are set, mistress. He will try to take you down by killing your mother or your mate. And when he tries, I fear that all will be lost if he should succeed."

"He won't. Not in taking my mate or my mother." She paced the small room and he watched her. He'd never seen such energy when someone walked. But she was walking hard enough that he was sure that the people below them could feel it. "What are your plans now? I mean, can you go back there and act as if nothing happened? Black will kill you should he find out."

"You will kill me first, so I'm not worried about him. I only ask that you make it quick. He will not, I'm afraid. There isn't a compassionate bone in his body. Nay, he will make me suffer in ways that will make what he's done to this poor woman look like child's play." She stopped pacing and turned to look at him. The fear that he felt was profound, and he held his breath for her to make the final blow to his life. But when nothing happened, he opened one eye and looked at her, and it was then that he realized she was confused. "You have every right to kill me, my lady."

"I do, but I'm not going to. Anything you might have done before has now been erased so far as I'm concerned, because you not only helped me, but you saved this woman's life. And you're going to be helpful in taking down Black." He was afraid and thought that she knew it. "This woman will be able to go on from here. I've taken away the memories of what really happened, and simply let her think she was raped." Bryce looked at the woman then, and so did he. "Not that rape is a simple thing, but what happened to her was horrific, and she might well have not been able to survive the memories of it. While not good, it will help her in the end."

"You're much kinder than any of us were led to believe. I think even the other witches, those that have had dealings with Black, believe you to be more monstrous than even him." Bryce nodded. "You will have much work to do if you are to have them trust you. And you will need their trust once you take charge of us all."

"I don't know if I want the responsibility of all that." She had started pacing again before he could comment. Not that he was sure what he would say to her. "I want you to stay here with this woman. I'm going to make arrangements for you to stay and see that she gets the best of care. For that to happen, I will name you as her husband. You will be Mr. Allen Burch for the time being. That is her last name. Her first is Kelsey. She will sleep for a bit longer, a couple of days anyway, until I can figure this out. Black won't know where to find you, so don't worry about that."

So now, here he sat, watching over a woman that might well have died had the grand witch not stepped in and saved her. Gray...Allen wondered why she had saved him too. As surely as he was sitting here, he was positive that if it had been anyone else that had done what he'd done, hidden what he had, they'd not only have been dead, but suffered greatly too.

Allen smiled at the nurse when she brought in his dinner tray. He'd not known what to expect, as he'd not had food for a very long time. He could eat, yes, but he'd long since lost the desire to have a meal. But when he opened the silver lid and looked down, his mouth did something that it had not done in more years than he could count. It watered.

"Is it to your liking, Mr. Burch?" He told her to call him Allen, and that it looked delicious. "Good. I was told to make sure that you have a good meal, and that I was to order it out for you. The rest of us are eating well too. Thank you for remembering us."

"You're very welcome. Since you're taking such good care of my wife, then it is the least I could do." He didn't have any idea what he'd supposedly done for them, but it had made this nurse happy. Allen would have to find out from Bryce what she'd done. "Do you think I could have a cup of coffee? I've sworn off of it for so long, but now I find that it's the only thing I can think about."

He used to drink coffee a great deal when he'd found out about it long after he'd started this job. But back then it was no more than brown water, sweetened, should he have wanted, with honey or syrup. He had despised both very much, so it was just brown water for him.

There was a story, one that he was sure was an apocryphal after all these years. But an Ethiopian man had discovered the bean when his goats would become very excited and full of energy after having a few beans of a coffea arabica plant in a nearby field.

When the carafe of coffee was set on his tray, he looked at it for several seconds before he realized that the nurse was speaking. She was asking if he'd like any sugar or cream as she turned the cup over on the saucer. Asking for both, he thought that he was going to try them all, after he took a sip of the most fragrant thing he'd ever smelled.

The taste exploded in his mouth. It was as if his tongue had been given a fine drug, his taste buds awake and raring to go after so long. Then he swallowed. The brew was hot, but that wasn't what made him moan. The flavor, the combination of it all, made him think that he'd gotten the wrong drink and not the coffee, the brown water that he'd asked about.

He'd been prepared for it to be bitter, to taste like nothing more than the smell. And even in that, he'd thought that he'd be happy. But that wasn't even close to what had moved down his throat like the softest silk as it moved over his body when he dressed. The warmth of it seemed to permeate his entire being—not just his body, but his mind as well. Setting down the cup, he was almost afraid to try any of the things she'd brought him for it and decided that he'd drink this cup and pour more for the second one.

Allen dug into his meal. The steak was magnificent— rare, just as he might have ordered it had he known how good it was. The baked potato was good as well, but when he discovered, quite by accident, that he could add the sour cream as well as the cheese upon it, he smiled at the way it all melted together to become a gooey delicious treat.

By the time he'd polished off the apple tart, what he'd read it was called on the receipt, he was so full that he wanted a nap. For about eight hours. Smiling, he leaned the chair he was in back and closed his eyes. He also felt safe for the first time. Safe from whatever nastiness happened at the WC office.

~*~

"Where did Gray say he was going?" White said that he

didn't know that he'd said anything other than "later" to him. "What do you mean, he didn't say where he was headed? He just took off? Without a word to anyone? I demand to know these things. You cannot just go flittering off like you have no duties to me. To the council."

"I guess he had something that he needed to do. I didn't know you wanted me to watch his every move, Black. He's a grown person and can take care of himself, don't you think?" Yes, Black thought, and he could also get them all into trouble. But he didn't say that. "I can tell you when he gets back if that'll help. But since I don't know where he is, I can't even know when he gets back. Maybe he's shopping. He seemed happy, that's all I know."

"For what? Who the hell would he be shopping for? I never gave him permission to do anything like that." White said that he didn't know but thought that he enjoyed it. And why did they need his permission to shop or enjoy anything? "That's not what I said. You enjoy just walking about, shopping? And what is it you shop for? A present, perhaps? Or do you just steal things and take them to wherever it is that you sleep?"

Black was in trouble here, letting his ideas spew from his mouth. Taking a deep breath, Black let it out slowly and inhaled once again to try his best to get his temper and his runaway mouth under control. But before he could speak, White got pissy with him.

"I don't steal. And I don't need nothing for my place. I can make it when I find it's something that I want." The indignation of the man made him laugh. "I don't know what you find so funny, but I'll tell you when he gets back. If he does. I'd not if I were him. You're just too mean all the time. And you're always thinking that you're the boss over us. You aren't the boss of anybody, Black. We're all equal, and you know it."

"I'm mean all the time, as you put it, because I have to watch over you two idiots so you don't get me caught...us caught when something goes wrong. As for being equal? You can't honestly think that you and I are even close to being the same. I'm much smarter than you and Gray together." White just stared at him and said that was why Gray kept a book. "I'm sorry. What did you just say?"

"Gray. He has himself a book that he writes stuff down in. I thought he was making himself stories to print up, but he said they were just doodles that he writes down so that if you had buried a body in a certain place, he was sure that you'd not use the place again. He wanted to make sure you didn't. What bodies? There something that I should know about?"

"I don't know anything about what he's writing down." But he did, and his balls, still sore from meeting up with Bryce, curled up again. "Just let me know if he comes back. Do you know where he keeps his book?"

"Yeah. They were all in this wall safe that he put in a long time ago. A really long time ago. And you should know that there used to be a whole bunch of them. I don't know how to count that far, but he's got a bunch of them." Black had started away, to toss Gray's room to find them, when White spoke again. It sounded to him almost gleeful. "But they're not there no more. He had most of them this morning when he was eating breakfast with me. He said that the rest of them are with a safe person. I don't guess he trusts us all that much. Especially you. He would have given them to you, huh?"

Walking away while White was still speculating on who was a safe person, Black went to Gray's home anyway. If he dropped even one of the books, he could find out what he'd been doing. It might have been just as he'd said, doodling. But for some reason, Black had a feeling that he was making notes on where he'd hidden the bodies, and all the other shit that he'd done over the years.

The safe, as if it were mocking him, was wide open. And there was an envelope on one of the shelves that was addressed to him. While he'd never seen Gray's handwriting, he was almost positive that the handwriting on it wasn't his, but that of someone that Gray had considered safe. Opening it up with trembling hands, he read over the missive twice before he sat down.

"Dearest Moronic Fuck." He didn't have to read the rest; he knew what she was going to do to him and who was saying it. But he did, reading it aloud for himself to hear to be assured of the words she'd put there. "This is the countess of Dragon's Keep, lady of Sheppard's Land, and the grand witch, Bryce Frost Farley. I wanted you to be assured who you were dealing with on all this. I am coming for your fucking ass. And trust me when I tell you, anything and everything you've done to the people that are buried across the world is going to be paid to you tenfold."

She didn't sign it. He supposed her full title and name at the beginning was quite enough. But the more he stared at the paper, the angrier he got. Who had appointed her the grand witch? Who but him could do such a thing? No one, that's who. It took two to—

Getting up, he went to find White. "Did you by chance sign anything that Gray gave you this morn? It would have been on very fancy paper." White was nodding before he could finish. "Do you have any idea what you've done? How you've hurt us all?"

"You mean making Bryce the grand witch? Nah, she said that I was going to be all right. Just so long as I didn't do what you were doing, and that I kept my nose clean. I've been washing it up every ten minutes to make sure. And that I was to come to her when someone asked me any questions. I could answer them if I knew what the answer was, but then I was to tell her anyway." He asked if she knew that he'd asked after Gray. "Well of course she does, Black. I just told you, I could answer you, but I had to tell her. She's my boss now. Ain't that grand? I mean, I'm going to get to go home now and have fun. I never had fun when I had to work with you all the time. Not that I didn't learn a lot, but I'm tired of it. And I get to keep my magic."

Magic. He'd forgotten about that. Going to his rooms now that he knew that the books were with her, he closed his eyes and tried to think. Trying his magic out should have been the first thing he tried, he knew that. But he was afraid that he'd been singled out, and that he was no longer as powerful as she was. If he'd ever been that powerful—and he was beginning to doubt that he ever was.

After twenty minutes of trying, he realized two things. He couldn't cast, but he could feed himself. Making himself a meal was the most menial task there was for a witch, and that was all he'd been left with. Apparently, she didn't want him to starve.

But, and he was so glad for this, he could still play with his magic. Which meant that he couldn't cast a spell by using books that belonged to him and him only, but he could use his magic to conjure. Most witches didn't know that there was a difference. And hopefully the new grand witch didn't know that either.

Almost giddy with relief that he could still kill her, he danced around the room. Then he made his way to Gray's room, destroying all the things that he'd left behind. Even if he returned now, which was doubtful, he'd have nothing left of his own.

Going back to his room, no longer concerned with trying to hide anything from the woman, he set up his plan that he'd been working on for a while now. Not being able to cast spells on the army he had thought to raise against her was holding him back, but he was using his magic to make all manner of things into monsters. His favorite was the stove that he had never used. The heat coming off it was hotter than anything he'd ever felt.

The table and chairs were now a scorpion looking creature. The bed, usually the most harmless thing that he could think of, was ready to take her on. The way that its pointy feet were stabbing the floor, Black could see her body under it, a mass of bleeding tiny holes.

As he worked on his new plan, he kept coming back to the books that White had told him about. Could they have been nothing more than doodles? Did he only want to have them published? Those thoughts were hopeful, he knew that. Gray had been spying on him all this time, and that wasn't right.

"Like I haven't done so much for him." He'd not, of course, but he didn't think that he'd done all that much to him that would warrant him keeping notes. And what sorts of things did he write about? "Probably nothing more than a few misdeeds. Nothing to get that upset about, I'm thinking."

But he was worried, and the worst part was, he had no knowledge as to what she was going to do to him now that she was the grand witch. Of course, he could just be paranoid about it. Likely she'd just give him the boot, as was her power, and that would be the end of it. But the note she'd left for him did say that she was coming for his ass.

"What can she do? Nothing. She cannot harm me because I'm supposedly a lesser witch than her." He thought about the books again. "Nothing more than a few things a day that would add up to nothing. For all I know, he could have been writing down that I'd taken a crap, or that I'd not showered daily."

Yes, he decided, that was all it was. Black knew that there wasn't any way that Gray would have known about most of the things that he'd done. The women were always hidden away in his lair until they were dead. And the money he'd been taking from the yearly fees that had to be paid by all the witches was stashed away in a place that no one would ever find. Even the pictures that he'd taken, the ones of his play, weren't anywhere that Gray would have been able to locate them. Black knew that he'd covered his tracks well. So well, in fact, that he couldn't remember all that he'd done in the decades that he'd been in charge.

Black hadn't ever been a good council head. He'd been a horrific person and hadn't grown into anything better as he got older. From the very start he'd figured out ways that this job could benefit him and only him. There was money to be had, magic that he could take, and women to be murdered after he raped them. Nothing was out of his reach, and he made sure that if it was, he'd get to it some way or another.

Now here he was, sitting in his rooms figuring out how to keep himself from being caught. Death wasn't an option, but she could destroy him magically. Black was going to work very hard on making sure that she didn't have what it took to take him down. Not when he had it in him to kill her first.

It took him most of the night to finish up his plans. Nothing would come between him and what he'd come to think of as his perfect set up. When he went to clean out his office and the other things that he'd had stashed, Black felt like a new man. And he was going to win this.

Chapter 9

Noah felt his dragon move along his skin. It usually happened when something or someone was scaring him. But Noah felt fine and wasn't the least bit afraid of the people around him. It wasn't until he stood up that he saw the reason for it. His dragon knew that it was raining.

Here, in this place, it wasn't necessary for it to be raining to let his beast out. But it was a habit now, and he went to the door to look out onto the wet grasses and the raindrops making beautiful circles on the pool water.

Noah was just stepping out onto the deck when he looked back at the pool. "We didn't have this before." He looked over at Bea when she laughed. "I love the idea of having a pool here, but we didn't have it before, did we?"

"No. Laura, she so loves to swim. And she's not been able to for some time now due to hurting herself a few years back. Bryce—she knew this, you see, and since she was worried for her mom going out and about with the council around, she put this in for her." He sat down on the chair that went with the table that hadn't been there before either. "Bryce loves the outdoors very much. I believe that she's out getting to know the grounds with William and some of the faeries. I'd like a word or two with you."

"All right." He relaxed, knowing that whatever she wanted or needed of him, he'd give it to her. "By the way, I've spoken to the school board, and they'd be thrilled to have you as a teacher here. I think they'd like for you to take over the art classes or the history. I thought you'd be a shoe in for the history department."

"I'd like that. Very much so. I'm not bored, but I do so love to be around children. They help us, did you know that? As a witch, we get some of their energy. Not stealing it, never that, but we can be fed from them." He knew that. It was the same for his dragon, but with trees. They gave him energy like he'd rested for decades. "What I'd like to talk to you about—I don't think that it's proper for us to be living here. Well, I suppose proper is the wrong word, but I think that Laura and I should have our own place. Behind the castle. Close, but not underfoot. I've already signed the castle over to Bryce, and I know that she's going to put your name on it as well, but we need a place that we can bicker in. We do that so well. It's why I love Laura so much."

"I don't think you feel that way, do you? That you're underfoot. Nor unwelcome." She shook her head and smiled at him. "Then you'll have to convince me why you should leave us. Not that I could or would stop you, but why? And so

136

you know, I am aware that there is no house behind the castle. There is nothing there but a stone mountain."

"Yes, well, if you'll allow it, there will be a pretty little home there for us." She looked at the pool before continuing. "Bryce needs to figure things out with you and not us. And while I know that you two talk about everything going on, Bryce is stifling her magic by being able to come to us when she thinks that she can't do something. She's powerful, Noah. Much more so than any other witch that I've encountered. And once we are out of her way, she'll grow into what she needs to be."

"The grand witch." Bea nodded, her pride showing in her face and smile. "I had to find out what that meant. I could have come to you or her, but I wanted to find out for myself. Besides, I think that Bryce would have given me the definition of the title. And you would have gone on about how proud you are that she is one, so I found out what I could on my own."

"I am quite proud of her, to be so young and now the ruler of it all. I could not have been more surprised that she knew how to go about it. But she'll need that, the magic and the title. Even though she's taken away some of the magic that Black has, it's still going to be a fight." Noah asked Bea if Bryce would be killed. "No. As I said, she's much too strong for that. Besides, I think you've shared what you are with her. And she has immortality now. As does Laura and me. Thank you for that."

"I would have thought that you were immortal before." Bea explained to him what they were able to do. "I see. You aged very slowly, but you would have eventually grown old and died. I don't want that to happen. I've come to love you both as much as Bryce does the two of you."

"Thank you, young man. I've grown quite fond of you too. You're a rare treat in this world—a man who loves with all that he is, and neither expects nor asks for anything in return." She picked up a pretty little tea cup and sipped from it. He didn't care for the brew most of the time but watched as the cup refilled itself. "But back to the house in the back."

"You have my permission if you need it. However, I think you should talk to Bryce about it. You don't have to tell her why you're doing it—though I would suggest that you do—but I would prefer that you tell her that you're doing it." Noah thought of not having the two of them around all the time. "You will need to come and visit us daily. And to have a meal or two with us weekly. I don't think you'll do it every night, but I would miss you otherwise."

"All right." She put down her cup and it disappeared. "Black is coming here. He has it in his head that because Bryce took away his casting magic, he's strong enough to take her on. I would hope that you'd be by her side when he comes calling. To show him that her animal to call isn't a cat, as he is assuming."

"My dragon would never allow anything to harm her." Bea smiled. "You know what's going to happen, don't you?"

"No. I know some of it, yes. But the outcome, no. There are many factors that could change it either way for him. Bryce will be fine. And she'll find her footing in the world of magic. But Black needs to be dealt with, and he needs to

138

be held accountable for the things that he's done. There are many deaths that he's caused for no other reason than that he could." Noah told Bea that he'd been going over some of the books with Bryce — the ones that were given to her. "Very good. Also, you may know this already, but Gray is now Allen Burch. The woman that he now cares for, she is Kelsey, and his mate. Bryce did that for the two of them. He will be working for her after this is finished."

"And the other man, White — what happens to him?" She said nothing. "Bryce said that he isn't fit to be on the council and is a person that is controllable — the reason that Black has gotten away with so much."

"He will live or die depending on the way things go. I know that it's a vague answer, but it's the best that I can give you." Bea kissed him on his cheek. "You're a good man, Noah. Your parents would have been very proud of the man you turned out to be. Even more so than they were before their passing."

He sat there for several minutes after she left him. Noah was proud of himself too. If not for meeting Bryce and her family, he didn't know what he might have done when arriving here. As it was, he was happier than he'd been in ages.

When his dragon stirred once again, he stood up and walked to the middle of the yard. Playing in the sky, that's what he needed. As he shifted, taking to the skies at the same time, he was pleasantly surprised to find not just Devon there, but his wife and grandmother too. They were having fun riding the winds that came off the mountain.

Flying over the castle's rear, he could see the house that had been put there. It was a strong stone home, with a chimney that would curl smoke from it in the colder months, and an herb garden that he could see even now was bursting with fragrance. Moving along the lake that was behind the house and through the mountain, he saw that the faeries had been working too. The trees that he'd brought here were standing as tall and straight as poles. Even the gardens by the mountainside were filling in nicely with the seeds that William had been gathering and saving since he came to be with him.

He'd picked his faerie just yesterday. She was a beautiful snow faerie, and her name was Snow. She joined him as he flew over the town, where the people were waving.

"Hello, my lord. I have a few things to tell you. I had thought that you'd come to me by now, but since you have not, I have found you." He could hear the tone she had but chose to ignore it. "The bodies that William and I have been assigned to find for Lady Bryce have been located. Their names have been put to the list that she has given us. There are a great many of them, I'm sorry to say."

Lady Bryce is now the grand witch, so she will tell you what she needs of you and William in the future. You are my faerie, Snow, but she might have a need for your services again. Snow said that she'd gladly help in any way that she could. *Thank you. And she will give you a bit more magic soon. I would say very soon.*

"I will find her after I speak to you." He nodded as he landed on the mountain top and stayed in his dragon form. Snow sat upon his nose so that he could hear her better.

"There is also a witch in the hospital that she has asked us to watch. I have several of the faeries that have come with you doing that. They are seeing to it that he is acclimated to being in the human world again as well."

Good. He is a good man and has been very helpful to her. I'm not sure what her plans are for him, but she will tell us when she decides. Snow said that she would be helpful to her when the time came. *I would like for you to find us a great many house faeries. There is some work that I'd like done on the castle. Also, Lady Bea and Lady Laura are building a home behind the castle. I want you to make sure that it is as safe as you can make it. They will require some house faeries as well. Staff too.*

"I will see to that." She pulled out a tiny notebook and opened it up. After writing in it, she turned to another page. "The mayor, as you may know, needs to be terminated. Lady Laura told me what that meant. They are hoping that you take the job. There is a great deal of work that you can do that he will not for the town. Most of it has to do with funding. Like the town the marquees is working on; there is a need of jobs and newer schools there as well."

I don't have the funding to help much right at the moment. She said that there was plenty of funding, but that if he didn't want to use it, she would make sure it was safe. *When my parents lost our home, they were broke.*

"Nay, my lord, they only lost what the accountant took. They had stashed away a great deal of funds for you in the belly of the mountain. I believe them to have passed on simply because they were tired of humans." He still didn't have anything to say. Well, he didn't actually know what to

141

say. "Shall I take you there, my lord?"

Yes. He stood up, then sat again and shifted to his human form. "With Lady Bryce. She's my mate and should be made aware.... Why didn't they use that instead letting the banks take it from our family?"

"I believe they knew that someday you'd return, and that the house would be in a stronger and better family. Your mother, she was brilliant in her way of thinking. I can remember her telling us all to stash away as much as we could from the home so that it might be yours again when you returned. It's there in the belly as well, my lord. All just waiting for you to ask for someone to take you to it. You have read their letter, have you not, sir?"

He'd forgotten about the letter his solicitor had given him. Taking the stairs three at a time, he went to where he'd put his duffel when he moved in. After pulling it out of the otherwise empty closet, he pulled out the envelope before sitting on the floor. Snow came to sit on his knee.

"Will you please find Bryce for me? Tell her that it's not an emergency, but when she has time, if she could meet me in the library." Snow said that she could do that for him. "Thank you. And then after we read this letter from them, you'll take us to see what they've put away for me, all right?"

"Yes, my lord. And if you do not mind me saying so, it is very smart of you to make sure that your mate is involved. It makes you a better man." Noah told Snow that Bryce made him a better man. "You are, sir. Even before you met the young miss."

He hoped so. For as much as he loved Bryce, he was sure

that whatever his parents said in the letter was going to make him miss them twice that much. They had been his world and his center for far longer than anyone else, of course. But they had shown him the wonders of loving someone and being loved by someone too.

~*~

"My dearest son, I'm so sorry that we cannot be there when you meet your bride. Bryce has been in our sights for a great many years. Her father, Austin Frost, was one of the only warlocks that we knew that was as kind as kindness can be. You will come to love her entire family, as we have." Bryce looked at Noah, who was sitting on the couch where he'd been when she got here. "They knew about us? They knew my father? I don't understand this. How could they have known that my grandma would buy the castle, and that we'd come here to live?"

"My mom, she had some ability to see into the future. Not a lot of details, but enough that she'd know this or that about something. Usually when someone was coming after us, or the outcome of a skirmish across the world. She didn't say much about it, but when she'd tell us to stay out of something or to invest, we took her word as gospel. Is that the end of the letter?" She told him there was more. "Please. Read it to me."

Nodding, she picked up where she'd left off. "We've had enough, my dear child. Not just of life, but of the way humans are treating our kind. Your father and I, we've decided to rest for a time. And when you grant us a child, we will return. Perhaps things will be better for us then." Bryce looked at Noah. "I didn't think we could have children. Is this her way

143

of saying that she'd not return?"

"No. I'm sure that she meant that any child that we bring into our lives, she'd think of them as her grandchildren. My parents loved everyone to a point. The breaking point would have been harming what is hers or what she considered hers." Bryce nodded and looked down at the letter again. "Bryce, would you like to raise children with me?"

"More than anything. But you do know that they'd more than likely have a rough time of it, having a witch for a mother and a dragon for a father. Don't you think?"

"So long as they're loved and know it, I think they'll be fine with whatever we are. And be proud of us so long as we make sure that they have knowledge and the wherewithal to deal with things that might come along." She nodded, remembering her own childhood being a witch. "Bryce, things are different than they were back home. People, mostly because of Devon and his grandmother, are much more accepting than what we had there."

"I know that in my head, but my heart has a hard time dealing with this. And now that I'm going to be in charge, all manner of things could befall them." She looked at him when he laughed. "You think that's funny?"

"Yes. Have you realized how much you've grown? You are so much stronger now than before you came here, I'd bet." She nodded and told him why. "No, it's not only because you've gotten more power. I think because you love and are loved, you have gotten much more confidence in yourself and your magic. Don't you think?"

"Yes, now that you mention it." She looked at the lovely

handwriting on the letter, and at the monogram that was at the top. A crest—his crest, she'd bet. "I want to have children. Lots of them. As many as we can afford."

"Good." He told her about the stash of things in the mountain.

"You mentioned that. When do you want to see it? After this?"

"Yes. Snow said that she'd take us there. I had no idea that she worked for the household when my parents were here." She said that she'd not either. "Read on and we'll see what we can figure out."

"Your father and I have left you our fortune in the mountain. I have instructed Snow when to tell you about it. We have also left you a great gift there—more than money will ever be able to give you. But you mustn't think that you should have children to bring us back, my dear boy, but to bring them to you when you are ready. We love you with all our hearts, Noah and Bryce." Turning the letter over, there was just a couple of lines more. "Bryce, you go to the meeting with that horrid man with my son. He is your animal to call, if you've not already figured that out. Such a smart girl, I'm sure that you have. But take him with you. It will end well for you both regardless of what you think now."

They gathered up what they thought they might need to go to the mountain, and when Snow arrived to take them, she took everything away from them and told them to follow her. They set off with nothing more than a large canvas tote to bring a little of it back.

"I have talked to the lady queen of faeries. She is going to

145

let us have a few of her people to come and bring the pictures and such back to the castle. Also, I have made arrangements, if you do not mind, to have the plants that were put to sleep awakened." Noah told her that was fine. "There is much there, things that have not been seen by any human or dragon in a great many years. Also, the eggs. They will be about ready now that you two have come together."

Bryce stumbled slightly. "I'm sorry. What did you mean, the eggs are about ready?" Snow stopped and turned to her. William was with her, and when he joined Snow, she asked them to have a seat. "No. If you don't mind, I think I might take this better if I'm standing. That way if I fall, I'm going to hit my head and be unconscious for a while. What eggs, and why are they about ready? Not to mention, how are they ready?"

"Over the decades, there were eggs laid by many dragons. In the time that there were dragon hunters, the eggs would be left behind—no one to nurture them, to make sure that they were safe. The lady and lord of the castle, they would gather such eggs up and store them away. For you." Bryce wished that she'd sat down when told. She was slightly dizzy. "My lady, are you ill?"

"Sort of overwhelmed." William touched her forehead and she felt stronger, her legs not as wobbly as before. "How many eggs are we talking about?"

Snow didn't look as if she was going to answer. And it was then that Bryce had a feeling that she didn't want to know. There had to be too many, a dozen of them, for Snow to not want to tell her. That was what she was going to go with.

Because if it was more than that, she wasn't going to be able to survive this.

"Let's just go to the cave or wherever it is, shall we?" Bryce could have kissed Noah. In fact, she needed to and did so. Holding her hand, he looked over at her. "This can't be as bad as whatever is going through our minds, right? I mean, how many children could be there?"

"Hundreds? My mind is in overdrive, so let's talk about something else. Do you have any idea how much it'll cost us to have to put them in school? And don't even get me thinking about college." Shaking her head, she stopped walking when the faeries did. "Are we there?"

"Yes, my lady." Snow looked hesitant. "You will help the town with this, will you not? They are in much need of many things. The school is in very poor shape. The library has not had a new book in a decade. The children, they are in need of a place to go to in the warmer months. Will you help them?"

"We will help them as much as they need, even if we have to go through all of this and get jobs." Snow smiled at them both. Noah glanced at Bryce before looking at Snow and continuing. "You make us a list of the most important things they need. After that, we'll do what we can until we have more money coming in. I promise you this on my parents' faerie garden."

The wall moved. Just as he finished with his promise, the wall of stone simply moved away, and the opening was revealed. The darkness was eaten up by light from the outside, but more of it was lit as the seconds passed.

Beyond where they stood, she could see snake like lines of

the light as it went through to each tunnel. It looked like there were at least four or five that she could see. Snow entered but waited until they joined her before she turned to them. The wall that they'd come through moved to close, closing off the outside world to them, and the only way that Bryce knew how to leave the cave.

"You will be safe in here. We must close the door so that no one, including animals, come into this place. If they should, they would surely die. There is no other way for them to leave, and there is no way for them to feed themselves." Noah asked Snow if it had happened before. "Yes."

That scared Bryce—just the single word, yes. How many? her mind wanted her to ask, but her heart told her to leave it alone. There wasn't any reason for her to know that others, perhaps humans, had ventured into this place while the wall had been opened up, and had perished while waiting for someone to return. Shivering slightly, Bryce followed Noah and the faeries, glad for the hand that held hers.

As they walked along, she wondered briefly how she was ever going to find this way again. There didn't seem to be anything that led a person along except for the light—light that she had no idea how it reached them, as there was no opening to make the path visible. Then she noticed something that she'd not before.

It wasn't light that was making it so bright that they could see where they were going, but gems and jewels in the stone. Bright diamonds, rubies, as well as others. Gold snaked along the walls, from one jewel to the next, as if it were powering the gems to be at their brightest. Touching one, simply because she could, Bryce could feel warmth from the stone, and ran her fingers along the path the gold had taken to make the lights possible. It too was warm, almost like a liquid heat. Taking her fingers away, she could see the film of the gold on her fingers, like she'd washed her hands in shiny dew.

"I think we're in trouble." She looked at Noah when he stopped. The room — the huge fucking room — was filled with chests of more gems; golden objects such as tea pots and cups; jewelry of all the colors of a rainbow. "It looks sort of like a pirate's treasure, don't you think? But that over there, that's what I was talking about."

Bryce stared at the corner. Making her way there, she kept telling herself it was the reflection of the gems making it appear to be more. The colors of the eggs, she was sure, meant something, but what, her mind couldn't narrow down. But touching one — just like before, putting her fingers over the first one she encountered — Bryce snatched her hand back when it burnt her, the heat boiling off it nearly hot enough to warm a house. Then she counted the eggs.

"There are forty-three eggs here. Forty-three dragon eggs. And we're supposed to raise them all at once? At one time?" Snow was speaking, but Bryce's mind couldn't keep up with her quick words. And Bryce was sure that she was speaking in her own language. But it was too much. Just thinking of the diaper bill was enough to make her ill. Then the ground came up and just slapped the shit out of her by hitting her square in the face.

Chapter 10

Black decided it was time for him to make a stand against this woman. He was sick to death of hiding in shadows, keeping to himself and trying to find Gray. No matter where he went or who he asked, no one seemed to have any idea where the stupid man had gone.

There had been no more contact between him or Bryce either. Not a single note. And nothing from White, for that matter. The hall where they would hold their sentencing for other witches was devoid of even a chair. And his dais, the one that he'd taken so much pride in making, was just splintered wood. Not even a single jewel that he'd forged into it was left in the place. He'd not checked, but he'd bet that all the light bulbs had been ransacked as well.

Trying to come up with an animal to call, he'd been thinking of all the creatures that he could remember seeing with other witches. He knew that Bryce had a cockatoo, her grandmother a lizard. Small things, he knew, was what every witch that he'd ever encountered had. Something that would, if necessary, lend to the witch some of its power, but nothing that would harm someone else if the witch was threatened.

The best he could come up with was a tiger, but it would be enhanced. And he knew now how make armor. Not for himself—he'd tried that several times—but for the tiger that he was going to make. The mice that he'd tried it on had been killed by his trials, but now he had it perfect.

Black knew the possibility of finding himself a tiger around here was going to be zero. So, he found a homeless man and changed him into one, which had been a great deal more difficult than he thought it should have been. But the tiger—a little off center at times, somewhat stupid others— seemed to fit the bill for what he needed. His tiger would eat the bird and the lizard, and he'd be home free. A show of strength, that's what he needed now.

Now all he had to do was bring her to him. That, he had no idea how to do. Since he'd been a council member, he'd only had to be present when the witches that had caused trouble, or what he had considered trouble, were brought to him. There had been workers for such a thing. Now he had to think where the books had been the last time he saw them.

"Damned grand witch. How the hell do I make us be in the same room?"

Almost as soon as the words left his mouth, he found himself in a great field, the witch in question standing there in front of him. Her mate, the stupid man who had shackled himself to her, was standing beside her.

"I'm glad that you called, Black. I think it is high time that we get this finished, don't you?" He nodded, and then stiffened his back and called to his animal. "A tiger? You didn't do him well enough. If you look there, some of his human is showing through. I don't suppose you asked for permission from the human to change him, did you?"

"I don't need to ask anyone for anything. I'm a witch of the highest quality. And you are right, it is high time that we finished this up. You aren't nearly as strong, nor as scary, as you think you are, young Bryce. And this will show you." He put his hand on his cat, the only way that he could put the armor on him and was dismayed that it didn't work the way that he wanted. "I haven't had this amount of power in some time. It's almost too much."

"Is it? Well, I guess we'll just have to see about that, won't we? Anyway, you have been brought before me to talk about all the crimes you have committed against other witches of your kind, and—"

"Wait, wait, wait. I'm not sure you understand. I'm far superior to you in all ways. If you would just give me a moment, I'll show you that I should and will have my job back, and you will...well, I'm afraid that you're going to have to die." She smiled at him, asking him why he'd think that. "For one thing, you have messed with the order of the way things are run. The council has a great many rules. And while you have broken only a few, the ones you have messed with, they are the ones that can get you killed. Now, I'm willing to cut you some slack, as they say, and only take one or two things from you in the form of payment. One of those, sadly, will be most of your magic. And your animal to call. Where is old Fred, anyway?"

"Fred has asked to be retired. And since I have found a new animal, I allowed him to go." Black told her that she wasn't allowed to do that either. "And why is that? There are no rules about anyone changing their animal. Why, I know for a fact that you have changed yours several times. That is, until I had to take him away from you for abusing the poor creatures. Did you know that they're just as we are? They need to eat and drink too. You left that little cat to suffer in ways that you shouldn't have."

"He wasn't what I wanted anyway." Waving her off, he asked her again where her animal was. She told him that she had no need to bring him out just yet. "Bring him out? When are you going to learn that you must have him with you at all times? My goodness. And you think yourself the grand witch? You're no more the grand witch than that man standing beside you."

"No, he's not the grand witch. And I do believe that he's all right with that. But I will have to tell you, Black, he certainly is enjoying the magic that was given to us. I am as well. I can do all sorts of things now that I never dreamed of doing before." When she put out her hand, he flinched. Christ, the laughter coming from her, the way she was making fun of him, made him see red. But he didn't let go of his temper, not yet anyway.

Black knew that it was important not to show too much at the beginning. Let her wear her magic out before he was ready, then he'd have a greater advantage over her. Not that he didn't already. She'd been remiss in letting him have enough magic to hang her with. Almost giddy now, he asked her again if she was willing to give up her magic to him.

"No. Why should I do that? It's not like you're going to be around long enough to use it anyway." Black asked her what she meant. "You know exactly what I mean. When you are read all the names of the people, humans, that you've murdered, then I will pass sentencing on you. You brought this all on yourself, Black."

"I did nothing of the kind. And I will be passing judgement onto you, Bryce Frost." She told him her name, all of it. "Yes, yes, I remember the titles. But those, as you said, will do you little good if you're not around to be able to use them."

He thought himself clever, turning her phrase back on her. Now all he had to do was turn his tiger into his fighting machine, ask her again what she was going to give him, and be done with her. It was really too bad that her mother wasn't there. It would have been wonderful to him to have killed the human in front of Bryce. Almost as if he'd conjured her, the very woman came from the tree line and stood next to her daughter.

"Hello, Black. I've come to see you meet with your sentencing." He asked the woman, Laura he thought her name was, what she was talking about. "I'm sure that it's been explained to you what you're here for."

"Yes. No, I called her here." He'd only thought of her and ended up in a field that was unfamiliar to him, but he wasn't going to be picky. "Listen, this is getting us nowhere. And believe it or not, I have many things to do today, and none

155

of them involve standing around while you make a decision. What will it be, Bryce? Am I to turn my beast on you? Or are you going to give up your magic and your mother to satisfy your misdeeds?"

"What misdeeds is it that you think I've done? And before you answer that, you should know that if you call your beast, or whatever that thing is that you've put together, I will call my own. And if I have to, you will never see another sunrise nor sunset. I will end you. It will be my pleasure." Black laughed. It was all he could do under such circumstances. "You think this is a joke? What is about to happen to you, you think that it's funny?"

"Yes, as a matter of fact I do. You cannot seriously think that you are going to take me over, Bryce. I mean, surely you have seen what my beast here is." He glanced over at the tiger and saw that it was sleeping on its back with its armor nearly off him. Kicking it in the side, it yawned twice before standing next to him. "He's had a rough night, tearing into witches that have broken the laws."

Black was looking bad. And worse than that, he had a feeling that he needed to regroup and come back at this another day. But there wasn't going to be any way that she'd allow that. And if she was in charge much longer, or her thinking she was in charge, then things might go badly for him. The end needed to come. Her end was all he needed to get himself back to where he'd been before.

"Armor, cover my monster." He watched his beast. The words transformed the tiger into a cat larger than his breed would have been. His armor, which had been strewn upon the ground, was now covering the beast's front and hind legs, his belly, and back. Black was quite proud of himself and what he'd been able to do in such a short amount of time. Looking over at Bryce, he watched her as she stood there.

Imagining what might be going through her mind, he had a moment of pure happiness. He'd outdone the so-called grand witch. And there was nothing from her — not even that old and worn out cockatoo had risen up. Yes, Black thought to himself as he took a step forward, this could not have gone better.

"Come to me, my dragon."

Black paused in mid step. His foot hovered above the ground for several seconds as he thought about what she might have said.

Dragon? There were no more dragons. And while he'd never had anything to do with the killing of them, he had been able to reap some of their amazing magic. Keeping an eye on his own beast, he kept waiting for the dragon, or whatever she'd said, to come forth as well. When nothing appeared, he figured, like most witches did when confronted with a bigger foe, that she'd lied.

The shadow across the lawn did nothing to make him believe. A cloud, he thought — the sun sliding behind a cloud to make everyone believe that she had a fucking all-powerful dragon. When his own tiger snarled at Bryce, showing more teeth than he thought he should have, he looked around and smiled at her.

"I see no beast, my dear. Perhaps this would be a good time for you to give up. I have pitied you long enough, and it is high time, well past time, for you to understand who is in—"

The great beast landed not four feet from him. He was monstrous, his body ten times the size of any car that he'd ever encountered. When he spread out his wings behind him, his tail became a mass of spikes that looked like he could fell an army. Then the thing roared out a flame of fire that looked like the earth was coming to an end. That the very idea of life after this was a pipe dream. After lying down, the great dragon beast allowed Bryce to put her hand on one of his spikes. The sound of his purring made the ground tremor and shake.

Regaining his balance, Black tried his best to think what he had to do next.

"Black, former member of the Witches' Council, I hereby, as grand witch of all, sentence you to death. The murders you have committed have been named, in accordance with our laws. If you wish a copy of the list of those that you have been found to have murdered, you may request it." She laughed a little. "However, as I said before, you will not be around long enough to use anything. Do you understand what you are being accused of?"

"I heard no names called." Bea, grandmother to the grand witch, stepped forward with a scroll, too long for him to read, and handed it to him. "When did you call their names to me?"

"When you were screwing around with that monstrosity you have there for your animal to call. Poor thing. Why did you do that to that human?" He said that he needed his own beast. "Yes, well, fat lot of good it did you. And the names

158

were called—I did so myself. I didn't care if you heard them, so I started at the house. You wouldn't know them even if they were standing here in front of you. So, yes, they've been called."

"I beg mercy." He knew that she could deny it to him. He had before for witches that hadn't done anything more than to have been a witch. "I beg mercy from the grand witch to give me a stay of execution."

"Nay. Dragon, kill him."

Black opened his mouth, trying to stay what was about to happen to him. But he was mesmerized by the sight of the beautiful dragon when he rose up on his hind legs, his wings spread wider than before, and inhaled deeply. Black thought it was the most beautiful thing he'd ever seen in his entire life.

~*~

Noah didn't say a word to anyone as he sat on the deck. The faeries were hard at work, trying to cover the burn mark that had been left by his dragon. He was also trying his best to get used to the separation of his dragon from him. In this, Noah thought, he was glad for it.

He'd seen dragons, of course. Not his own, but his parents', as well as a few of his friends'. But to be witness to the one that had been his, that was still his, as he killed a man was so surreal that he wasn't sure what to think.

Noah looked up when Devon came to sit beside him. He liked this man, a great deal. Devon didn't need to fill silences. He was smart, articulate, and he had a good sense of humor. What he didn't have was tolerance for stupidity or cruelty; nor did he suffer fools well. Black fell under the last category very well.

"The queen came to see me. She asked me if she could fix the grounds that had suffered this day. And she asked that I send your wife her love for ending the world of the monster." Devon looked around. "Where is she, anyway? Bryce, I mean."

"Did you know that when a witch is murdered and no one is caught for it—the person responsible isn't held accountable for the crime—they don't leave this earth until the murderer dies or is finally held up for his crimes?" Devon said that he hadn't. "Bryce is with her grandmother, talking to the families of the victims. Another thing that I wasn't aware of. Once the witch is freed from their bonds of death here, their family is given some kind of signal that tells them that things are all right now."

Noah looked out at the field again—really a part of their back yard. It was the safest place they could be. The only place, really, that his dragon could have come out as a beast and not scared anyone that might be close by. He didn't bother looking at his friend but talked like he wasn't there at all.

"My dragon lives in me. He's there should I need him. But the moment that Bryce needs him as her animal to call, he is no longer a part of me, but is a beast that is forever in his armor, and much larger and stronger than the one that I am." Devon made no comment, for which Noah was grateful, so he continued. "He's blood red. I don't mean a really pretty shade of red, but like warm blood that has just left a body. His spikes—and he had a great many of them—are tipped in poison. And when he blows his fire, say over someone's head as a warning, he doesn't burn a thing. Not a tree, a bush, or even a blade of grass. It's like he knows better or something. Like he needs to protect the earth from himself."

"Are you afraid of him?" Was he? Yes. Yes, he decided, he was very much afraid of him. But he also knew that he'd never harm him and said that to Devon. "When he's not a part of you, do you feel lost? Like you've lost a great part of you?"

"No. It's like I can still feel him inside of my body. Know that if he needed me, for any reason, I could shift and be some help. He's me—mine, I guess you could say. Without me, there would be no him, and the other way around if it came to that." The faeries seemed to have finished up their work and were all gone but a few. And by few, he meant that there were only about five dozen rather than several thousand. "I'm Bryce's animal to call. I have all this magic that I didn't before. And I just, as the beast, murdered someone."

"Did he deserve it?" He looked at Devon and asked him what he'd said. "This man that you supposedly murdered, did he deserve it? Or did you just kill him because you could? Valid question. What's your answer?"

"Yes. He'd killed—murdered—several hundred people over his lifetime. Even before he worked his way up into being the head council member. Some of them humans, most other witches. Did he deserve to be killed with a dragon though? That's the question that keeps going round and round in my head." The pop to his head was hard, pushing his forehead so far that he hit the table in front of him. He looked at Lady Susanna when she joined them. "What was that for?"

"Are you finished feeling sorry for yourself, Noah?" He said that he wasn't. "Weren't you? Where is your wife right now? Your mate? Is she here wallowing in self-doubt? Is she sitting here with her whiny mate, feeling sorry for herself because she ordered the death of a man that didn't deserve to be breathing in the first place? No. She's out there, telling mother, father, sisters and brothers, aunts and uncles, that their child has peace. That the bastard that killed them, simply because he had the power to do so, is dead. Yes, I can see where you'd be so pitiful that you'd have to call on your best friend to come here and hear your woes. Poor Noah. His beast did just what he needed to do, and—"

"That's not fair. She—" Susanna stood up, her stature looking twice that of herself, her anger palpable. And it was directed right at him.

"You do not get to interrupt me when I'm having a conversation with a child. And that's exactly what you are acting like, Noah Farley. My goodness. Why don't you wait here, Noah, so that I can run to the store and pick you up a binky and a diaper so that you might take a nap?" She smacked him again, this time on the cheek. "Get ahold of yourself and find that mate of yours and help her, before I take it upon myself to help you along. And let me tell you buster, if I have to *help* you along, it's going to be a long time before that beast of yours feels comfortable enough around me that he'll even peek his head out. Get up off your ass and get to helping Bryce. Or so help me, young man, I will—"

He cut her off with a kiss to her cheek. After telling her how much he loved her, how he was glad that she'd not taken his shit, he left both Devon and her sitting on his deck. Their laughter followed him all the way to the open field and beyond, him shifting and taking to the skies.

He felt better than he had before sitting down with Devon. Noah thought he felt better than he had in decades. Flying over the town, where she was going to start her trek, he found her sitting in a small children's park that was in just as much disrepair as he'd ever seen.

Making sure that she was alone and that there were no children around, he shifted back about two feet from the ground and made his way to her. Bryce smiled at him when he sat on the sagging broken bench.

"We need to get this repaired. I'd be terrified to send one of our children here, and they'll be immortal." He told her that it needed to be dozed over and started new. "Yes, I guess we have plenty of funds for that. And children to come here and play."

They'd not spoken of the stash of funds, gems, jewels and other things, nor of the eggs. She freaked out about it every time he tried to talk about it. But now, she seemed as ready as she'd ever be, and he opened his mouth to ask her what she wanted to do when she started talking.

"I talked to Snow. She's very knowledgeable, by the way. She said that we only need to bring out one or two of the eggs at a time to hatch. They'd be called hatchlings. I guess you'd know that. And since we're going to be raising them as our own, all we need to do is tell William what we wish to call them, and he'll take care of the paperwork." He asked her what else she wanted to know. "I'm taking this as I can

163

handle it. I mean, I'm overwhelmed, but not like I was when I counted them. And before I forget, Susanna said that she knew some people that would help us convert the stuff in the cave into ready cash and teach us how to use it. I don't know really why we'd need help with that, other than having it fenced."

She leaned back on his shoulder when he put his arm around her. "They're not called fences when they're helping a dragon. I don't know if you're aware, but we can really make tears when we need to. To be honest with you, I just never thought of it as being a way to make me rich. Susanna told me a few hours before Black showed up that most of what was in the cave was from all the other dragons that my parents were able to help by taking their children. Not stealing, she assured me, but hiding it so humans would not find it and take it apart."

"And we'll make sure that it's used for other children as well." She handed him a drawing. It was crude and not to scale. "I was given that when I sat down, by a little boy who said that someone told him to come to me. I'm assuming that it wasn't a faerie?"

"It more than likely was. Children can see what adult humans cannot. And when they see these little people, as the faeries enjoy being called, parents think that the children have imaginary friends." She nodded, and he looked over the picture. "I guess he wants a new playground set. It's actually a very good drawing."

"It is. And I'm going to be working with Kelly on the same kind of projects she's working on in their town. We're going to be putting in an after-school place for kids to go when they have working parents. Also, bringing jobs here." He kissed the top of her head, telling her too that he loved those ideas. "Noah, do you think that we should wait on our first egg? Or should we just do it now? Either way, I don't know what to do. I want a child, lots of children, but I haven't the slightest clue how to raise a dragon."

"When hatched, they're dragons — smaller versions of me. But once they reach about one or so, not too much past two, they can become human. It helps with their upbringing to be able to interact with humans, these humans nowadays, as much as possible." She said she could see that, but how did she feed them? "Well, they eat on our legs and arms, whatever we can spare at the time. Then when they get a real taste for meat, we let them feast on an — Ouch, that hurt."

She had pinched him, hard, on the leg. Noah couldn't help it, he was still laughing as they made their way back to the castle. Bryce said that she'd put out there that if anyone needed to speak to her, to contact her. She would come to them or vise versa. They entered the quiet house and made their way to the living room. It had been a long day, and they were both exhausted.

Chapter 11

The meeting was finally here. Bryce was getting highly pissed off every time the guy in charge, Mayor Fuzzy Head, told her to sit down. That wasn't his real name, of course, and she cautioned herself, once again, not to call him that out loud. Mayor Harold Fritzburg was a fuzzy headed ass, and she was going to zap him if he didn't let her speak this time. Standing up, she waited for him to call on her or to tell her again to sit. This time she wasn't going to put up with it.

"Mrs. Farley, we have gone over this again and again with you. There is an order to meetings, and you just have to wait your turn." She just stood there, counting to one hundred so she'd not lose her temper. Again. "Now sit down, honey, and when—"

"I do not shit honey out of my ass. Your Honor." She paused just long enough for him to realize she hadn't forgotten his title but didn't care. "I am here to talk to the townspeople about getting a—"

"I've had about enough of you and your interruptions, miss. And if you do that again, I'm going to have you arrested." She pulled out the town's committee book, one that Susanna had given her. When Noah touched her back, she felt his reassurance, and that was all she needed.

"I have been to four of your so-called meetings, Mr. Mayor, and the children of this town aren't going to be any safer when they go out to play." He opened his mouth and she glared. "Say one word and I will not be responsible for what might befall you. The children in this town deserve a better playground. Better equipment to play on. Certainly safer for them. My husband and I would like to start up a fund to make it happen."

"Good for you. And if you threaten me again, you will be thrown out of these proceedings and barred from ever coming here again." She told him that he couldn't do that. "Can't I? Well, since I'm the one in charge, then it stands to reason that I can make the rules. Especially ones regarding you. Now sit down and—"

"I, for one, would like to hear what she has to say." Devon stood up. He was technically not a part of this community; his town was just one over. But he carried a great deal of weight all over the world. "What is it you'd like to propose for the children, *Lady* Farley?"

"Thank you, Marquess Wakefield." The room began to softly mummer, and she turned her back to the mayor and began her spiel. "The equipment at the field is rusty. The swings have large places in them that could seriously injure a child. And since this is the county's grounds, then they'd be the ones footing the bills for the child. Also, the other equipment is of ill repair. There is only one way in which to fix it so that they'd have a good place to go, and that is to take it all down and begin anew. My husband and I will pay for the funding for the equipment, as I've tried to say several times over the last month. But the townspeople would have to help in having it put in."

"My daughter was there just last month with her two little ones. My grandson, he got himself a nasty cut on the slide. I swear, it took it nearly a month for it to heal. And he still has some trouble with that." The man looked at the mayor. "When I proposed to you that there was new playground equipment needed, you told me that the only way to do that was for me to pay for it. Then you wouldn't even see to it that his bills were taken care of. I, for one, would be glad to help put the equipment up and get it running."

The room erupted in horror stories about one cut or another. One child had broken his arm when the swing he was on had broken. The gavel that was on the dais kept pounding and pounding, but no one paid it any mind. And almost every person that had a story to tell volunteered to help with the construction of the equipment. There were other things on her list, a great many of them as a matter of fact. But she'd take this one victory and let the others go for now. Bryce had a feeling that she'd not be dismissed so easily from now on.

Mr. Phillips, the first man who had stood up after Devon, came to see her after the meeting. Mayor Fuzzy Head had left about half way through the meeting in disgust. She shook his hand and introduced him to Noah.

"I've been thinking on that playground equipment that you wanted to donate. That's very good of you, but there are other things that this city could use. I don't mean for you to donate it all; no, that's not what I'm saying. But there is something that you can help us with." She asked him what it was. "The high school kids had this thing they used to do when I was going to school here. They'd go out to the elderly home and do crafts with them once a week. The money ran out for that about five years ago, and I'm thinking that the kids and the elderly sure miss it."

"A few crafts doesn't sound like it would be overly costly. What is it you're trying to tell me, Mr. Phillips?" He grinned, and she smiled back. "I'm not one that beats around the bush to get to the point. I'm more of a beat the bush into submission and get what I need to know."

"She is at that." Bryce looked at Noah when he spoke. "But your way, it's so much faster and easier to believe. Tell her, Mr. Phillips, what you believe is going on with the funding."

"The mayor, he's got him an awful lot of toys for a man that only makes about fifty grand a year. That's not to say that he has to live in poverty. No. The mayor position has a lot of perks—insurance, housing, as well as a car and staff. So that's the reason for the seemingly low pay. But he has himself a yacht." Bryce tried to think what that had to do with the funding when it hit her. "I can see your mind working. And so you know, I have an idea what the two of you are. I knew the Farley family when they were alive around here. I was sorry to see them go. But you, you're a witch. And if I

170

don't miss my guess, a fairly strong one too."

"I am. But this mayor thing. You think that he took the funding for the crafts just to fund himself on a few extras. I don't see how that's going to pay for a big boat. Unless the funding for the swings for the kids was used as well." He only looked at her. "I see. And this funding—how much, just a guess if you don't mind, has come up missing?"

"One point seven million dollars, and some change. That's not all, either. Last year the school was supposed to have a library put in. New books, better seats for the kids. And a few extra computers for them. But, and this is according to him, the money was taken by the person in charge of it. The accountant. And no one has seen hide nor hair of him since. I'm thinking, and this might just be me thinking aloud, that he's taken the money and disposed of the accountant too."

"And you think he was a part of it. Or had someone do it for him." She didn't have to hear his answer—it was written all over his face. "What is it you wish for us to do? I'm sure, like me, you have a list, a plan, and people that you know are involved with him."

"You're a smart cookie, aren't you? Yes, ma'am, I have a list." He handed her an envelope, with his badge there on the top too. "Federal Agent James Phillips at your service. We're here from the US to take him in on deaths that occurred on our soil. If you don't mind."

"Why not just go in and do this on your own? Unless you don't want to blow your cover because there is someone higher." He told her there was no one higher that they knew of, but he really didn't want to blow his cover, not on this.

"And after I find this, whatever it is, what happens to the townspeople? They're already left holding the bag, so to speak. And they're losing more every day."

"I'm going to take care of that too. But in my own way." She didn't know what his way was and was almost positive that she didn't want to. "You figure this out, give it all over to me, and I'll take care that he's getting what he deserves. But, if you could see your way to helping out the elderly, I'd be very beholden to you. My mom is in the local nursing home here. She was born here in the UK. And all she talks about is how bored she is. She fell and broke her hips some time ago and isn't able to live on her own anymore. And doesn't much care for my home. It's not all that big anyway."

When Noah and Bryce made their way home, they decided to stop by the school. Not to check on the story, but to find out what sort of things were needed to make the crafting possible. And while they were there, the principal and the janitor—a man as old as the building, she was sure—were trying their best to put buckets in all the rooms that were leaking from the recent rain.

"I'm so very sorry, Lady Farley, but it's been a heck of a day. And with school starting in a few weeks, we're not sure how many classrooms we're going to be able to use." She asked for a tour. "Yes, of course. But I have to tell you, it's a mess. A real mess right now."

The school was in worse shape than she could have imagined. They were still using chalk boards that had been out of style for a great many years. The desks were a hodgepodge of tables with mismatched chairs, and it looked to her like they had very few of them. The closets that the children used had some doors on them, but for the most part, they were broken pieces of wood that someone had propped up against the broken glass windows. By the time they made it to the cafeteria that also served as a meeting room, she was convinced that they had to start here.

How long do you think it would take to build a new school? Noah asked her if she knew the faeries could do it. *No. I mean, I know that they can do a great many things, but build a building? Actually, I don't care. Whatever it takes so that the children can have a place that they don't have to worry about the roof falling in on them. Our children will go here, and I am terrified that by the time they're old enough to go, this building will be in less repair than it is right now.*

I'll make a few connections. You and I, we promised to make a difference, and this is the right thing to do. Also, you should add this to your list of things to look into. I can't believe that this hasn't been on someone's list of shit to get done. She told him that she would. *All right. But I swear to you, honey, if the other schools are like this one, I'm going to hunt that man down and burn him to a crisp. This is uncalled for.*

Bryce wanted to hug Mr. Potter. He was trying so hard to make the place look good by talking it up, but there wasn't anything much to talk about. Everything in the place needed to be fixed. Most of the teachers' desks were nothing more than a long table with scratches and dents in them. And one of the teachers had a stool for a seat. It was horrific.

When they left the school, having donated what was needed to get the crafts started, Noah had some answers for

173

the school build. He'd even contacted Devon and a couple of other friends of theirs to help out. The faeries were as excited as they'd ever been for a project. Now all they had to do was figure out a way to make it happen in the shortest amount of time possible.

They also made a stop at the elderly home, looking in on Mrs. Carter and getting her list of things that she'd like to craft. The home wasn't in any better shape than the school, but at least they had better food for the people there. The inmates, what Mrs. Carter called them, had taken over the kitchen about six years ago, and they'd never eaten better.

"And so's you know, that mayor, he needs to come here and stay for a week or so. Just to see what he's done to his poor mom." Bryce asked where she was. "In a bed. He has the nurses keep her out of it so that no one knows that she's related to him. A little touched in the head, but I remember her from when we lived on the same street. She's a nice little bird, but she needs to not be so doped up all the time."

Going to see her was hard to make happen. The people there were loyal to Fuzzy Head. She thought perhaps he was paying them off. But when Noah threatened to make a few calls of his own, not only was she able to see the woman, but she was given her chart as well. Things were about to get all hairy for the dishonorable Fuzzy Head, Bryce thought.

~*~

Fourteen hours after they had their tour and the towns meeting was over, not only did they have a blueprint that had been made up last year, but they had the land prepped as well as the first workings of getting a new grade school in.

174

A new high school was also being built, but it was more the conventional way—for now at least. Noah looked over the things that had been given to them at the meeting.

"You said that at one time you were an attorney." Noah looked up at Bryce as she continued. "What do you have to do to update that? I'm sure that it's not easy, but perhaps it would help us along on other projects."

"I have a valid license now. When my parents were starting to lose the castle, I made sure that I could help in any way that I could. Fat lot of good it did us. What do you have in mind?" She sat on his lap, a sure sign that he wasn't going to like whatever she was going to suggest. "While I think this is a great position for sex, I'm not going to be persuaded to do whatever you're going to ask with you fully clothed."

Bryce pulled her top up and over her head. Her breasts were bare, and he leaned down to take one of them into his mouth, but she stopped him. His head was hurting from where she held him there with her hand full of his hair.

"Will you be mayor?" He shook his head. "I'll let you have your way with me. And not only that, I'll suck your cock every time I come to visit you in your newly appointed offices."

"You don't play fair; you know that, don't you?" She let him go, and he lifted both her lovely warm breasts up and suckled them both into his mouth. "I believe, my dear, this would be considered blackmail. What a way to start off being mayor for this fine city."

"Noah, you could do a great job. And if someone pisses you off, you could— Oh yes, that's it. I love it when you're greedy like this." He was having a good time with her breasts, but he really wanted more of her. All of her. "What if I told you that Mr. Phillips has put your name in the hat for the job when this is done?"

"I'd say that you pushed him into it, and that you'll have to pay for that." He made them both naked, and watched as she stroked his hard, aching cock. "You keep that up and I'm going to come all over you."

"I don't care how you come so long as you take me with you. I want you to be inside of me, Noah. I need you more than I thought." He lifted her up and slid her slowly down over his cock. "Oh, you feel so good like this. I don't think I'll ever get up from here."

"I'd like that. However, I don't think we'll get a lot done, do you?" She kissed him, her tongue making his feel like they were dueling for supremacy. He pulled back, but only far enough for his mouth to run down her throat to her breasts. Noah loved his mate and thought about the rest of his life with her. "Marry me, Bryce. Please?"

"Yes. Now make me come, Noah, or I swear to you, I'm going to do some serious damage to your perfect bod." He smiled at her and stood up. When she cried out, not from pain but anticipation, she told him, he put her down on the floor and bent her over the desk. He had no idea why he liked having her this way in this room, but it was certainly fun to hear her scream.

As soon as he entered her, she did scream her release. Slowing himself down, Noah took his time touching every part of her back. The muscles along her ribs. He gloried in the way her arms and shoulders held her body up. When she turned to look at him, Noah saw her muscles tense up; her pussy around his cock did as well.

She came three times with him being as slow as he could go. Sweat poured down the center of his back. The way that she was holding onto his desk, he wondered if it would forever be marked by her nails. And when he leaned over, nipping none too gently at her shoulder, he felt his own balls tighten up and then empty deep inside of her.

When she pulled away, her body nearly as glistening with sweat as his was, she told him to take her again. Bryce sat on his desk, her legs open wide, and pulled him toward her. He didn't even pause but slammed forward hard enough to move the desk again. When she came, digging her nails deep into his arms, Noah came twice more, each time filling her until he was in pain. Christ, he loved his woman.

Sitting down, keeping her wrapped around him, he leaned forward and pulled open the top drawer. Taking out the ring that he'd unearthed in the cave, he slid it onto her finger and was so happy that it fit. Looking up at her when the sparks from the light danced over her body, he told her how much he loved her.

"I think the ring was part of a set. Snow seems to think that the rest of it, a necklace as well as a pair of earrings, are in the treasures someplace. When I asked her if I should use them for you, to marry you, she said it was just what they were intended for. To wed a man and woman who were in love." Bryce said that she did love him. "And I love you, Bryce. And yes, I'll take the job of mayor when it becomes vacant."

"It might be a bit sooner than we thought." She gave him a rundown of what she'd been able to unearth. "Most of the stuff that we've been able to find are big ticket items. And here's the thing—if he was taking money from the pots around town, and there is no reason to believe that he hasn't been, he has also received a tax refund every year since he took office. I don't think he's supposed to do that. But I'm looking into it."

When Bryce got up and dressed, he did as well. As soon as they were both suitably clothed, she went to the door and called for Allen. Allen had been Gray on the Witches' Council. Noah asked about his charge.

"She is going to be living with me for a time. The missus here, she found me a place to live, furniture, as well as some food. I've not ever shopped before, so she made sure that we had all we needed. Kelsey, she has no one else but me, she told me, and we're going to make a go of it." Noah told him that he was happy for them. "Not nearly as happy as I am that I was able to help out to get rid of Black, sir. He was bad news for a great many people. Lady Bryce told me that he paid his dues. I'm pleased for that as well."

It appeared that Allen was going to be working with Bryce as her assistant. There was a great deal of paperwork that she was to fill out when something happened, and Gray was very good at it, Bryce told him. So, it was working out for everyone. Kelsey would work for Noah, as she'd always been a secretary before being hurt by Black, and he had a feeling that as mayor, he was going to need as much help as he could find.

The rest of the evening was spent going over paperwork, chasing down creditors, as well as finding out all the things that had been purchased by Fuzzy Head, a name that Noah thought suited him perfectly. After supper, not only did they have a good lead on where some of the money was going, but also an accounting of where all the funds had been taken from.

"The building is about ready." Noah asked Snow what she meant. "The grade school is nearly finished. We have also found the teachers that will be working in the building and found out what sort of supplies they might need in the way of teaching. I had no idea there were so many things that humans would need to learn."

"Like what? And I got word that you and your men are also working on the high school. Thank you for that, Snow. You are doing this community a great service by helping them out." She told him that it had been their pleasure. "I got word, too, that the construction company that is being used is going to start planting a fruit tree with every build they have. Usually they plant a maple, but now they want to plant fruit trees that will grow in this area."

She looked very pleased, and Noah was glad that he could help Snow with that. He asked her again what sort of things she'd been told about from reading the teachers' minds. Snow smiled at him.

"Allen has helped us a great deal as well, sir. He will need to be able to speak faerie before much longer. I can do that for him, but I should like to have Lady Bryce's permission. She did save him." Noah said that she could ask her. "I will. Thank you. But the things that we were to find were computers. They were most difficult for us. They differ from company to company. But as I said, Allen helped with that. We have also given each class an endless supply of markers, paper, and tissues. Those are things that they run out of quite frequently."

"Were you able to find anyone that would want to cook for the schools? I know that I said we'd only need a few, but I've heard that they might need as many as fifty on staff. Not all of them want to work full time, so we're dividing the work up so that a lot of part-time people can work if that will help." Snow told him that she had several that were excited, and some of the brownies wanted to help as well, but not with the cooking. "Good. We'll need staff to clean up too. They'll work with that should they want to."

They had a lot of teachers applying for work at the new schools. Some of them were human, but for the most part, they were shifters. Wolves, bears, and cats could also keep the children safe from any kind of intruders if they were to encounter any.

When she left him, Noah had a better understanding of the school system. Snow had gone above and beyond the call of duty on this, and he was going to have to reward her in some way. All the faeries were helping them so much that things were looking up.

"I just got a call from Phillips. Man, that man is slick. Anyway, he said that he was showing his boss what we've been able to put together. He's very impressed that we were able to do this in such a short amount of time." Bryce grinned.

"I guess this has been in the works for several months, and until today, all they had was speculation on some of what we found to be real. But they're going to make a move sometime today or early in the morning. And when I told him that you were throwing in your hat for the job, he said that he'd like for you and I to be there, along with Devon. Apparently, he's been trying to get them to do something about the man for a few years."

"All right. When will we have narrowed down time to do this?" She said that Phillips was supposed to call them, but they might not have a great deal of time to be there. "So, we're to just drop everything and be there?"

"Pretty much. The only thing that I know for sure is, they have gotten into a couple of accounts he had. Nothing overseas, as they thought he might do. In fact, mostly he's been spending it as quickly as he could pull it out of some account. Bastard." Noah asked what was going to happen to his toys. "They'll sell them off and put the money back in the places he took it from. I don't think they're going to get as much as he paid for them, but it'll be a start anyway."

Yeah, Noah thought, a start. But he had a feeling that wasn't going to be the end of it. They were going to find something bad about the guy. Really bad. He hoped not, but he didn't have much faith in men in power, especially human men in power.

Chapter 12

Devon sat at the desk. He'd never had the ambition to be any sort of political member, but he could see that Noah would make a good one. He was just the right kind of person to make a difference in this town. And this one needed someone to start helping them out.

He'd gotten the pictures of the old school just this morning before leaving his home. No one had come to him about it — he wasn't really sure why. Devon thought that a great many people thought him to be like his father had been. But he'd taken great strides in trying to be his own man, and nothing like the bastard that had sired him. If not for him, Devon knew that his mother would still be alive.

But he had his grandmother, mother to his mother, and she told him stories all the time about Mom when she'd been a child. And the antics that she pulled would have surely gotten him killed had he tried that with his sire.

Devon never called him Father. He either referred to him as his sire or the bastard. Both were true. Devon had never hated anyone as much as he had his father and killing him that day was the best thing he could have done for a great many people. Especially for himself and his grandma.

"You should have a party." He looked at Bryce and wondered if she could read his mind and asked her. "I doubt I'd be allowed in your mind, but no, not this time. I was thinking about the school. And the people around here. I'm sure that you would have gone out of your way to make sure they had everything that they needed, and then some."

"Yes. I have a great deal of time and funds to do a lot for a lot of deserving people." She told him that she and Noah did now as well. "I heard. My faerie has been here since my family first built my home. Snow and mine are very good friends. I believe they are from the same spring time harvesting."

"I was told that. I think the queen might have told me, or Snow. Anyway, I bet that not many people are aware that faeries are born with the first blooming of the flowers. And that the ones that aren't collected, they become fully grown as faeries that can be in the human world. But they have to be either or. They cannot switch once they chose to be in either world." She grinned at him. "Back to this party. Not so much a party, but a feast of the fall. Witches celebrate every season at some point or another, but the fall one, All Hallows Eve, is our favorite. You should have a fall festival. That way everyone gets to know that while you can be a bad ass, you're usually a nice all-around guy. Noah is hoping that with him being mayor, if he gets the job, he'll show people that even

184

though he's a dragon, he's a nice guy too."

"Believe it or not, Kelly was just saying that we needed to do something. I showed her the pictures that you sent me. Thank you for that, by the way. And the faeries, they were so happy to have some hand in helping too." She nodded and asked him if he'd seen the new grade school. "No, but that's a splendid idea."

"I'm sorry. Did I miss something here? I only asked if you'd seen the new school." Devon nodded. "Noah does that too. Doesn't answer me, thinking that I'll understand. Do you want me to hurt you? I can, just so you know. Not kill, I'd never do that, but I can hurt you a great deal."

"Nay, you love me too much to harm me. Remember, I'm a nice guy too." She snorted, and he laughed, making them the center of attention. Waiting until they were back to what they had been doing, he continued. "What I meant was, a grand opening of the new school. Have a feast in the new digs, and perhaps sell some crafts. The locals would love that too. And, the kitchen will get a nice run for its money. And I'm very happy that they won't have to cart in meals anymore. I heard that some of it, while nutritious, wasn't all that hot or cold when it should have been."

"Yes, I heard that too. I think that's a splendid idea. And with the interviews going on with the new teachers, we might be able to have a couple of the rooms set up and have a get to know the teachers thing. Also, you know, I'm sure that they've found a new principal for the high school and the grade school. The middle school one decided to stay on. And Noah approved it after they did a very deep background check on him."

They talked about different things that were going on around town. A couple of them he was going to see about taking care of in his own little place. The two towns were reasonably far apart, about twenty miles, so doubling up on some of the things going on around here was going to be all right.

"I had a phone call the other day. I haven't any idea why they thought to call me, but they were asking if you had opened up shop here. I didn't know what they meant. So, in my way of making sure that your privacy is kept, I told them to fuck off." They laughed again, and he decided that he really enjoyed this woman's company. Kelly and her were a great deal alike. He asked her what it meant.

"I'm a witch. And now the grand witch. Because they didn't have any idea who you might be—though why they'd call you I don't know either—they wanted to know if I had set up a council. I'm not, in the event you ask. There doesn't need to be three anymore, as I'm the only person that can pass judgment on witches and warlocks." She looked at him then. "I need to rent—and I really do mean rent—a building from you for court. You have to rent it to me, because if you ever have to be before me, if you know any witches, then they cannot say that you have been paying me off. I doubt that would ever happen. But that's one of the rules that we have."

"All right. I can do that. Why my town? Wait—because it's supposed to be neutral, correct?" She nodded. "Is this going to be hard on you, Bryce? Passing judgement on others of your kind?"

"I don't think so. I mean, it might be if I know the person well, but I'd like to think of myself as being a fair-minded person. Someone that likes rules for what they are but doesn't have any trouble bending them if it calls for that too. Just not to the breaking point." He agreed with her. "That's not to say that I won't have trouble, however. There are people out there, like I thought you were, that think rules are made and they're never to be broken. But I have since changed my mind about you. You really are one of the good guys, Devon. A person that can be trusted and trusts easily. But once that trust is taken away, it's not something that you'd give again."

"My sire. I think you've heard about him." She nodded, and he did as well. "It would be difficult not to have heard of him. He was a bastard and a cruel thing. Not a man. He could never have been considered a man, good or bad. He was just evil."

"Did you really knock him down the stairs and wait until you were sure he was dead before you called for help?" He nodded, afraid that she'd judge him for that. "Good for you. I think I might have done it long before you did, but you did have other people that were depending on you. Also, before I forget again, you grandmother, a wonderful person by the way, is with my mom and grandmother planning mine and Noah's wedding. I'd be honored if you could give me away, since I have no one that I like enough to ask. Other than you."

With that, she got up and walked away. Devon sat there for several minutes, his mind as blank as his calendar for the day. When the sitting mayor came into the room, he was on the floor and screaming about his rights before Devon was

187

able to get up and move. He felt like he'd just been given the greatest honor someone could bestow on him — to walk his friend's bride down the aisle.

"I would like to know the meaning of this." The agents, all of them in flack jackets, just kept reading him his rights. "I know damn well what my rights are, and — What the fuck is she doing here? If this is about that meeting, we have rules and she simply wasn't willing to abide by them. My word is law, and she just acted like it was all about her and some damned playground for the kids."

"About those kids; what happened to the money that had been earmarked for the new schools, the better busses, as well as the elderly home having heat and air? Also, the food is subpar, and the —" Mayor Fritzburg cut Noah off, telling him that the funding had gone to new roads and newer parking meters along Main Street. "Really? The roads are in worse shape than they were before my parents passed away. There aren't any parking meters on the main street or anywhere else in this town. Try again. Or should I just tell you? You have a nice boat that you bought. Also, a very lovely home that… well, I should say that you used the money to have those things."

"What the fuck does that mean? I bought that with my own money. I have all the receipts at home for everything I bought." Noah told Fritzburg that would certainly make it easier to figure out how much he owed the city. "I don't owe them a fucking thing. They paid me to take care of them, and I did a fine job of it. At least up until you and that woman showed up. Now I have people coming out of the woodwork asking about this or that thing that I promised to get done. I did what I could for the ungrateful people around here. They should have taken care that they had those things in the first place. Besides, what do you think is going to happen now, boy? You think that just because I supposedly took a little here and there that anyone is going to care?"

"I would. And I do care. My children will be attending those schools that you neglected. Did you know that there is only one working bathroom in the place?" He said that the boys could use the trees, that's what he'd done as a boy. "And I guess that in the winter months, that'd be fine with you if they were to get sick and not able to attend."

"You let me out of this, Farley, and I'll make sure you can use my boat whenever you and the missus want. Also, there isn't any reason for this to get out. I'll be a better person about the money. Might even be able to work around a way to pay a part of it back. Not too much of it though. I have needs too. And that is the fault of the city too. Should have paid me more if they wanted someone honest in the position. I'm not admitting to a damned thing, but that's the way I'd be thinking."

"Oh, I think I might have forgotten to mention something. You were warned, I know, that the agents here are recording everything that happens, but the news people are also here. Several of them from all over the United States. You did a number of murders there as well. My lovely missus, as you called her, thought it would be a grand idea to have someone here that would be witness to your comeuppance." Fritzburg looked around, then back at Noah. Even from where he stood,

Devon could see the anger on his face. "Want to wave at your taxpayers, Fritzburg? I'm sure that they'll have plenty of good things to say to you if they get to see you."

Devon was positive that the former mayor was making a few of the curse words up as he went along. And when he was pulled up from the floor, he was shackled at his ankles as well as his wrists. Devon was going to have to see if Kelly had heard of a *twittering food trough mage detector* before. And of all the things he was spewing, his favorite might have been an *animal-fondling clusterfuck infidel*.

As Fritzburg was being taken off to jail, Noah was sworn in as temporary mayor. There would be a vote in a few months, but by then not only would the town be in much better shape, but he was sure that Noah and Bryce would have met every person in town to find out what they needed in the way of improving the city.

Devon was glad that he'd gotten to witness both events. The arrest of a terrible man and the swearing in of a good friend and ally. Noah and Bryce would do great things, and he was going to have to make them let him help. Laughing, he made his way to his car. It was time to get a start on a few of the things that Bryce and he had talked about.

~*~

Noah had the entire office that he was to use cleared out. He wanted nothing from the other man even to be near him. All of it was donated to the local shelter, where their next project was going to be starting. He was just getting the floor measured for his desk when Snow joined him.

"We have a gift for you, my lord. All the faeries have

190

gotten together to make you this." He thanked her and told her that it wasn't necessary. "But it is. You know the faeries and know what we need. You will not destroy our gardens in the name of a parking lot."

"He was going to do that?" She nodded. "Yes, well, I won't. We need more beauty in the world and less concrete. It has its uses, and I couldn't be in a home that hasn't used it in some way. But just to be tearing something up to replace it with the hardness of that is just ludicrous. What is the gift?"

He really loved giving gifts. Christmas was, to him, a time of the year where he could really go overboard. Not that he didn't year-round, but he knew that their first Christmas together, he was going to have so much fun buying for Bryce and his new family.

The money that he'd be making as mayor would be for extras. Going on a vacation. Out to dinner. They had enough now that he had the stash, and Snow had assured him that he could use as much as he wanted now that he'd fulfilled the agreement that he'd had with the stone. That had startled him the most.

The mountain had known of the troubles. Not only that, but with all the things going wrong in town, no one had come out to see him, hike on his walls, smell the pretty flowers, or view the trees. It had made him stronger, this love the people had for him. But when hard times had come along, people were working more and getting out to do fun things less. He wanted the promise of the things he held so that he could be just as healthy as the town would be for it.

"You must stand back, my lord. If you are in the way, you

may be harmed." He asked what she was doing. "You will see. It is the most wonderful gift I have had a part of giving to someone. And you deserve it, and so much more."

The room tightened, and he felt slightly sick as he sat in the window box of his office, a place he had planned to fill with herbs and plants. Noah closed his eyes against the fast-moving things in the room. Bright lights were there too, so bright that even with his eyes closed and his head buried between his knees, he could still see it.

"My lord, you can look now."

Noah slowly raised his head and opened one eye. He still didn't feel well, and when he saw the room, he nearly leapt out of the window seat and onto the desk that was sitting in his office.

It was perhaps the most beautiful thing he'd ever laid eyes on. Every piece of wood was of a different type of tree. He couldn't name them all, but he did recognize birch, as well as oak and pine. Running his hand over the wonderfully smooth surface, he marveled at the size, the pattern that had been inlaid on the top, as well as the pulls on the draws, also wooden. Sitting down, he looked around the rest of the room.

There was a filing cabinet in one corner, made the same way, which shone beautifully in the sunlight. There was also a flat credenza that was covered in a thick piece of glass—he supposed for plants and such. While he was looking around, he could see that he had a new braided rug, just like the one that was in their bedroom at home. And turning when Snow asked him to, he saw that they'd made him blinds. They too were made of different types of wood that reflected his tastes more than he'd thought possible. Even the place where he'd been sitting, the window box, was now covered in the same style of wood.

"This is too much." Snow told him that it would never be enough for him. "I just don't know what to say. I love it. Every single piece that has been made for me."

"Pull out the top drawer and looked at the bottom piece." He pulled the door open and wasn't surprised when it slid out easily. "See the hand prints? Those are from every one of the faeries and brownies that helped make this for you. The other drawers have the same markings too. There were too many to simply put on one piece of wood."

Running his fingers over the tiny hand prints, he wondered aloud how they'd put them there. She told him that they had used the juices of the different trees to stain the wood, and that after it was finished, they were there for him to see. Looking closer, he could see their marks alongside their names. It was in their language, but he could read it as well as any book on the shelves at home.

Bryce joined them a few minutes later. She too had a gift for him, but she said that it was nothing compared to the furniture. Pulling her to his lap, he held her while he pulled the tissue paper from the bag. It was his name, proclaiming him as mayor, on a piece of fine oak. The other gifts, she told him, were from her mom and grandmother.

The desk set too was made of wood and looked as right as rain sitting on the desk. He thanked the faeries for what they had done before they left them and told them that he wasn't going to place any concrete where it wasn't necessary. And

193

as far as he was concerned, the only place the stuff should be used was houses, parking lots that were necessary for a business, and headstones. And if anyone said any differently, they'd need the latter of the three for themselves.

Bryce helped him hang the pictures that he'd brought from home. One of them was a painting of his parents, the other of the castle. He knew the artist that had done them for him and doubted that many would believe who it was. So, saying nothing, he smiled when stepping back to look at them there.

"I have had the faeries bring two of the eggs to the house." He asked her which two. "Like I'm supposed to know that. A yellow one and a dark blue, almost black one. I suppose you know what sort of dragons we'll get from them."

"I do for the yellow one. She'll be a smaller dragon, not much bigger than a full-grown horse. And she'll be a family dragon, which means just what you think—it can breed. Also, and this is something you should know—dragons aren't born a sex. They adapt to whatever is necessary in the area that they are in. So, our dragons will more than likely be females, until such a time as a few others come to find them." She asked how that worked. "When there are a few dragons around, they sort of call to each other. Not when they're older, but young ones, less than two hundred years old."

"Yes, well, to me that's not so terribly young. And the darker one. How do we tell what it's going to be?" He said that Snow more than likely knew, or William. "I'll ask them when we get back to the house. There is a child at the hospital in town. Her parents were drug addicts, and she's been fighting off the drugs since she was born a few weeks ago. The doctor that called told me that she'll have some issues, but not too many, and none too severe. I'd like to take her in."

"All right." She turned to look at him, and he could see the confusion on her face. "Did you expect me to tell you no? We talked about this, having children, and the dragons won't be hatched for a while yet. And even after they're hatchlings, they don't need much care from us. Just some fresh meat until they can hunt for themselves."

"What about humans? Will they try and have them for a tasty meal?" He shook his head and told her that humans weren't all that tasty. "I was going to ask you how you knew that, but I don't think I want to know."

"I don't know. Not really. My parents might—they've been around for a very long time." She asked him if he'd found their garden. "Yes. Snow and William took me to it yesterday."

"And so, we have to wait for one of the eggs to hatch before they come see us?" He said that he honestly didn't know. "Before I forget, again, Mom and Grandma are all moved into their home now. They want us to come to dinner one night. I assured them that we would. And since I forgot to tell you about it, we're going tonight. I'm sorry."

"That's fine. I didn't have any plans anyway. When do we get to go see this little girl? And when is it she can be released from the hospital?" She said they had time to go now if he wanted. "I can see that you really want to do this. Let me lock up here and we'll head there. Who else knows about this?"

"I didn't tell anyone in case you didn't want to bring a

child into our home just yet. I mean, we've already moved out my family, which I hate and love too." Noah laughed, saying that he understood. They were close enough should she want to see them, and far enough away when she didn't. "We're going to have to go shopping for stuff if they let us take her home today. We don't have a stick of children's furniture, and not even a big enough car should we need to put a car seat in it."

"Snow and William can help us with the house. I mean, look what they did for my office. And I think they'd be thrilled beyond words to have an infant in the house. Babies give off a certain kind of magic all their own."

They were getting into his car when he realized she was right about the car. All they had was this little two-seater, and when they needed to be someplace different at the same time, one of them would have to walk. It was time that they both got them something reliable, as well as large enough to carry their child in—as well as groceries and such.

They made their way to the hospital while talking about the child. She was human, which didn't matter to either of them, and she might have problems. None too big, Bryce had been told, but issues all the same.

"We can fix that. You know that, right? I mean, whatever the effects of the drugs were on her little system, we can use a little of our magic to make whatever is wrong gone." Bryce asked him if he'd let her do that. Noah thought she had been thinking of it but had been slightly insecure about it. "Yes, that would be wonderful. It'll be hard enough growing up with dragons as siblings. Anything that we can do to give her a head start is fine by me."

The hospital nursery was busy. Sixteen babies had been born in the last week, and they were trying to keep them all fed and changed. When they were asked to have a seat in one of the rooms, he could tell that this was going to be epic. And when the nurse came in, pushing the little cart, he stood up at the same time Bryce did.

"She's had her bottle but will need another in an hour or so. I've done as you asked, missus, and have only been feeding her when she's hungry and not on a schedule. So many parents use the timing method these days." Bryce told her that her mom said to do that. "Well, she's a good person then. The child has no name, not even a last name as yet. The doctor has cleared her to be released today. Just need a little more paperwork and she's yours."

"Can we hold her?" The nurse flushed and told them they could. She'd forgotten that part in trying to remember the other things. "Marquess Wakefield, he said that he called and gave you our information?"

They'd told Devon only that they were thinking of adopting a newborn, and that the hospital required a reference for it. Devon and his family contributed a great deal to this hospital, so his was the only reference that they needed.

"Yes, yes, the doctor knows Lord Devon as well. All right then, here you go. Your daughter, should you want her."

Bryce was first, and as soon as she started crying, Noah knew they were leaving with this child, even if he had any reservations about it.

He didn't. With one look down at the beautiful face that

stared back up at them, he fell head over heels in love with her. Bryce asked him what his mother's name was.

"That's lovely. I love it. Lily. Her name is Lily Stafford Farley." Bryce looked at the nurse and repeated the name, telling them that was the baby's name as well. "That's about the best news I've heard in a very, very long time. Let's take her home, shall we?"

It wasn't as easy as that; they had a lot of stuff to get done now. But having a child, their child, with them was going to be so much better. He was glad now that they'd stopped to pick up a new SUV before making their way here. Thankfully, the hospital gave them enough supplies, including a car seat, to start out with. Noah wanted to shout to the world that he was a dad.

Chapter 13

Bea was waiting on them when they returned. She had some things to tell them, and she wanted to tell them the first thing when they got home. But when they pulled out that little car seat, everything in her head seemed to have flittered away. My goodness, she thought. I'm a great grandma.

"Oh, look at that face, will you? Such chubby little cheeks." Bea touched her fingers to her face even before they got her out of the car seat. "Laura, just look at that little girl. I swear, you and I are going to have some fun now."

She knew that the child wasn't healthy. Giving her just a little magic would help, but she also knew that Bryce was stronger and would help the little mite along. Drugs—her little body was as full of them as an addict's. Bea asked what her name was.

"We named her after Noah's mother. Lily Stafford Farley. It seems only fitting, since she knew that we were coming

199

together." Bea didn't even feel jealous. There would be more children, and a few of them would be named for her, she was sure. "We've got our name on a list now that says that we'll be willing to take any newborn they have come in that's been abandoned. And children, from time to time, that just need a little extra care and love."

"Lily. What a lovely name. Oh, and such a beautiful child." They'd taken off her blanket and sleeper to look her over. Bea had never been so satisfied in her life. The little girl was perfect. "You didn't let us know. I should be upset, but I can't be."

Them letting Laura hold her first had nearly made her mad, but Laura was a new grandma. But Bea didn't go very far, looking at her watch every few minutes to try and be reasonable about how much longer she had to wait. It was much better, she supposed, than just snatching the child from her arms and running off with her. But she had company, and—

"Oh my goodness. Your parents are here." Both Noah and Bryce looked at her. "They're over at our home—they came about an hour ago. I completely forgot. Let me go and get them." Noah said that he would, if she didn't mind. "No, no. You go on ahead and I'll be here. I cannot believe that I forgot them. But then it's not every day someone becomes a great grandma. Laura, honey. I've tried to be nice, but if I don't get my hands on that little girl soon, I'm going to bust."

Laura handed the baby to her. "I did wonder how much longer you were going to wait. You lasted a bit longer than I would have, I think."

Bea just waved her off as she peeled the little blanket off her very first great grandchild. Lily stared at her like she was just as curious of her as Bea was of Lily.

"Well, you're beautiful, aren't you? And such long fingers. Before you know it, Grannie is going to have you casting spells all over the place." She looked at Laura. "You and I have some major shopping to do, I think. Is this blanket from the hospital?"

"Everything we have is from there. We did stop and get a new car though. But the car seat, and even that small diaper bag, was given to us. Noah and I were hoping that we could pick up a few things on the way back, but we just wanted to come here and show her off." Laura said that she was so happy for them both. "Oh, you should have seen us when they handed her over. It was like my heart had just been waiting to be filled up by her."

Bea thought that was the sweetest way she'd ever heard to describe having a child around. They did fill up a person's heart and, most of the time anyway, became the center of attention. But there were others, like this little girl's biological beings, that needed to have been shown the error of their ways. But they did have little Lily out of it, so she would be all right with them still being alive. For the moment, anyway.

Bea thought about Noah's parents. She'd had a nice long conversation with them before the kids got back. She wanted to see what sort of people they were, what they thought of him marrying a witch. They were much nicer than she'd thought.

People had children all the time that were very different than each other. She knew of one couple that had five boys,

201

all so different from each other—not only in looks, but temperament—that she'd often wondered if their mother had had affairs. Even if she hadn't, it mattered little to them. They raised their children up to be kind, loving, and careful. All but two of the boys did as they'd been taught.

The oldest boy was about nineteen when he decided to try and outrun an arrest. He and a couple of his buddies robbed a store at gunpoint and ended up killing one of his friends as well as the worker. The police chase had ended badly. Two others were killed, one of them the officer, when the boy had rammed another car and killed a mother of three.

She didn't know where the second boy had fallen in the family, but he was far worse than his older brother—murdered his parents and siblings when he'd not gotten what he'd wanted for his birthday. She didn't remember what it was, but it hadn't been that much.

The baby yawned, and she looked down at her. "You are getting into the best family, I hope you know that. You and I are going to have such fun." She closed her eyes a little longer each time she blinked. "My precious little baby girl. I'm so happy that you're here. I already love you to pieces."

When Bryce sat down next to her with a bottle, she handed her over. How could she love something so tiny so quickly? Bea wondered. When Bryce put the bottle into her little mouth, she knew that it was a distraction. The child was sound asleep and not taking any of the formula.

"Do you suppose they'll like me?" Bea asked her who. "His parents. Noah has been gone a long time. Maybe they're telling him to get rid of me or something."

"Bryce Frost. Where on earth did that come from?" She shrugged, and tears filled her eyes. "Honey, I'm sorry. But they already love you. I talked to them before you got home. I cannot believe that I forgot about them. Anywho, I talked to them and they are very nice people. And since the faeries were watching over them, they already knew about you. They don't know about the baby."

"They told us, in a letter, that they'd come when their first grandchild came. I'm wondering if that was why they came now." Bea told her that it was because their son was so happy. "I hope you're right. I'm worried."

"You shouldn't be, honey. They really do love you. And if they don't, then I'll take care of them for you. Dragons or not, they will not do a thing to my granddaughter that gives her one second of grief." Bryce laid her head on her shoulder and told her that she loved her. "I love you so very much, Bryce. You make me prouder with every breath you take. And I will forever be happy with this baby."

"She is beautiful, isn't she?" Bea asked her about the drugs. "I've already taken care that they're coming out of her system slowly. I don't want her to be in pain by removing them all at once. She'll have withdrawal symptoms, just like an adult."

Bea hadn't thought of that and was glad that she'd not totally healed her. They heard the door open in the back of the house and she felt Bryce tense up. Patting her leg, she took Lily from her and drew a shadow around her. That way, if Noah hadn't told them about the baby yet, then Bryce could hand her over to them. This sharing thing was going to make her insane before more children came along, Bea thought.

Noah hadn't told them. As soon as he introduced them to his parents, Thomas and Lily Farley, he then brought Bryce to meet them. Instead of waiting on Noah to do that, Lily grabbed Bryce up and hugged her like she'd missed her. In a way, Bea thought that they had. Missed their son finding his one and only love.

Bea wondered when they were going to talk about the baby. Surely they would at some point. But when it became apparent that they were waiting for some sign, little Lily yawned again and let out a little cry. Letting go of the darkness around them, Bea laughed when both Noah's parents just stared at the bundle in her arms.

Standing up, Bea handed the baby to Noah. It was only proper, she thought, that he do this. And when he pulled Bryce to his side and handed her the child, Bea was as proud of him as she was her granddaughter.

"Grandma and Grandpa Farley, I'd like for you to meet your first grandchild. This is our daughter, Lily Stafford Farley." Noah's mother started crying and reached out gently to touch the child. Bea stood by—if they hurt either of them, she really would end their lives, dragon or not. Bryce started crying as well and handed Thomas the baby. "She has a few issues, but we're taking care of them slowly. I thought that was why you showed up today."

"Oh my, no. We could feel how happy Noah was, and we just had to come and see you. But this little thing, she was a complete surprise. You must have been planning this for weeks." Noah told them that they'd gotten a call today and gone to get her. "She can't be that old, is she? The little thing. I'm in love with her already."

"We are as well."

Thomas handed the baby to his wife, who sat in the rocker that hadn't been there before. Bea had no idea who had put it there, but she was glad for it. And then she remembered that the baby had nothing to sleep in and nothing in the way of clothing.

"Lily, my daughter, Laura, and I were just heading out to get some things for the baby. All they have are a few things from the hospital. They had no time to get anything of her own." Lily looked up at her, hope written all over her face. "If you'd like to come with us, we'd surely be glad for it. I mean, since we're going to be family now, we need to bond over shopping, don't you think?"

"I'd love that." She kissed the baby on the cheek and handed her back to her husband. "I've not been shopping in a good long time. Do they still have department stores around?"

"I thought we'd head to one of those baby specialty shops. They have everything under the sun for a child. And she'll need diapers and such as well." Laura was putting on her coat when she asked Bryce for a picture of the formula they were to get. In ten minutes they were all three loaded up in the car before Laura asked them to wait a moment.

When she came back out of the house, she had Bryce with her. It had never even occurred to Bea to invite Bryce, thinking that she'd...well, she had no idea what she'd been thinking. But she was glad that she was coming too. They'd make an evening of it. Bryce even remembered to invite

Kelly, who was so excited to be invited that she said she'd meet them at the store. This was going to be epic, Bea thought. All them women converging on a baby store with their credit cards out. They'd be lucky if they could fit everything in the car. Then she remembered that they had faeries that could help them out and doubled her mental list of things to get. Yes, Bea thought, this was going to be more fun than she ever dreamed, having a baby in the house.

~*~

Noah sat with his dad while he rocked Lily. He didn't say much to him—Dad wasn't one to talk a great deal. But he was having a nice one-sided conversation with the baby. Noah was still trying to wrap his head around the fact that he was a dad.

"Dad, do you think that you will stick around, or will you go back? You know, wait for a dragon to be born." He had no idea why he blurted that out, but his dad just smiled at him. "I'm slightly overwhelmed at the moment. We have two of the dragon eggs that you left us in the basement. Not sure what we're to do about them hatching, but Snow has it under control, she told us."

"No, son, we're here to stay. And Snow is a wonderful faerie. She'll do right by you." Noah nodded. "Would it be all right, you think, if we hung around here for a few days? I don't know much about buying a house, but we wouldn't want to crowd you two."

"You won't stay here for good?" His dad laughed, and Noah realized that he'd squeaked a little with the question. "I'm sorry. But I'm sure that Bryce would love for you to live here with us. Her mom and grandma did for a little while, just until the faeries helped them with a home. They live behind us."

"I know. It's a wonderful little house. Much like the one you had in town before coming here. It's a good deal larger on the inside." Noah told his dad that he'd shown them what magic to use to make that possible. "And the lovely things they have in there too. Bea said that the faeries have been very busy helping them out."

"They have been us as well. I'll have to take you to my office downtown. By the way, I'm going to be mayor. Well, I am mayor, but only until election time. The past one—you remember him—was taken away in cuffs yesterday." Dad told him that he was proud of him. "Thanks. Did you know that Bryce is the grand witch?"

"Take a breath, son. You're overwhelmed-ness is showing." Noah did as his father said and felt better. "Now, slowly this time, tell me how your lovely mate made it to grand witch at such a young age."

He told his dad everything that had happened. And when Devon showed up, they greeted each other like long lost friends. Which, Noah thought, they were. Devon's grandma had been a good friend of their family for a very long time—long before Devon had been born and his mom had been killed.

"I cannot believe what a handsome man you turned out to be, Devon. My goodness, when you were just a small boy, I thought for sure that you'd be dead before you were twenty-five." Dad flushed. "I'm sorry, son. I sometimes let my mouth get ahead of my manners. Your father, he wasn't the nicest of people."

"No, he wasn't. And I don't call him my father. He was my sire. I was raised by the staff, and then Grandma when he was killed." Dad apologized again and showed him the bundle. "You and Miss Lily have a baby, Mr. Thomas?"

"No, no, this is Noah's little girl. Lily, after his mom." Devon looked at Noah. "He and his little mate, they're going to take in more children like this little girl. The hospital, Snow told us, has them on a list to help them out. I have to tell you, Devon, they'll be helping this old man out more than Noah and Bryce will them. But isn't she the prettiest little thing you've ever seen? And I'm to understand that you and your wife are having a child as well."

"Yes, in seven months. Kelly, she has my mom's dragon." Dad looked shocked by that, and Devon went on to explain. "She said that she was waiting for her, Kelly, to have a place to live. It's wonderful having another dragon with me when I fly."

They all three talked well past seven, and Noah realized that they'd missed having dinner with Bryce's family. He was hungry too. When asking his dad and Devon if they were, it was as if they only just then realized how late it was. They too were starving.

Since the women were out shopping—a scary thought, Noah realized—they decided to go into town too. So, instead of getting the cook to make them something, they decided to meet the women and have a nice meal. Lady Susanna was going to join them as well.

The ride wasn't that long, but Noah realized how much he needed a bigger SUV like Devon's. Just having the car seat next to him in the back was tight, and his car was the biggest one he thought he needed. No, he realized, they'd need a semi at this rate.

They were going to have more children, that was a given, and hauling them around everywhere was going to take some work. And room. Learning what he needed to do to figure out what to take with them was going to require a list each time.

"You're thinking too hard again, son." He laughed with his dad while he told Devon how quickly he'd been shooting out statements earlier. "I thought his poor head was going to come off."

"I'm going to be watching Noah and Bryce closely, I think. That way when they mess up or figure something out, then I'll have a heads up when our child comes."

Devon drove with ease into town. And by the time they had a table, the rest of them showed up. It was going to be loud and fun, and he was looking forward to it.

Kissing Bryce, he asked her if they'd finished. She rolled her eyes at him and he laughed. "Did it not go well? I was thinking that the way you were all armed with cards, you'd have finished up by now."

"We nearly emptied the store, Noah." He thought she was joking. "I'm not. We have so many things in the back of the two cars that we brought that it'll take a month for us to sort them all. And let's not get me started on diapers. Did you know there were as many kinds of diapers as there are brands?"

"No. I'm assuming from the look on your face that you didn't know what to buy." She glared harder. "Okay, why don't you tell me what happened, so I can go and slay them all for you."

"Keep that up, buddy, and there will be a snake in your bed. This woman, and I'm not being nice about it, went through every kind of diaper there was. I mean, every kind. There are swaddlers, one through about twenty, and then there are swimming diapers. Of course, I took that to mean, you know, they're fixed so a baby can swim and not drown. No, they're for the baby not to be able to pee in the water. So, my statement to her was, but after the diaper is wet from—well, both—the pee still ends up in the water." He laughed. "Yeah, she didn't think that was so funny. My mom did. And Grandma. They were both crying they were laughing so hard. But I couldn't tell if it was from what I said, or the expression of total disbelief on the woman's face. She was pretty pissed. And I'm sure if we'd not spent a large fortune in the store, she would have had us escorted out."

They were seated right away, mostly due to having Devon with them. He was a big deal to these people, like Noah wanted to be to his own little town. And ordering was a nightmare, he was sure, for the waitstaff, but they took it in stride and smiled the entire time. Noah was sure that at one point he would have thrown up his hands and walked away. There were just too many of them with different tastes to be an easy order.

"I was wondering something." He nodded at Lady Susanna. "Didn't you and Devon have a few friends in college?

I mean, other dragons? I was wondering if we should, now that we have eggs and children to protect, invite them here to help out."

"I don't know. Most of our dragon friends were having their own set of issues when we were there together." She asked him what sorts of trouble. "Well, there was this one buddy, Jackson was his first name." When he couldn't remember his last name, he asked Devon.

"Jackson Williams. He had a castle that was destroyed about the time that my mother married. I think he lost a sister and was quite bitter about it." Lady Susanna asked Devon if he'd rebuilt. "Not by the last time that I heard from him. He was...let me think. I think he might have been set to marry, to converge two lands or something. She was killed in battle, if memory serves me. Jackson had a lot of bad luck. Still does, I think."

"He was stripped of his title too. Something about his father siring several daughters and having them killed." Bryce looked at him, shocked, and Noah explained. "It doesn't make it right, but a great many lords did that to females born to them. I think that there were several of them, and since he couldn't marry them all off to bring him more land and money, he simply killed them. I'm sorry, but that's the way it was."

"It's a good thing that I wasn't born back in those days. I might have had to murder a few fathers in their sleep." Snapping her fingers, Bryce brought up an image that danced above the table, showing a man sleeping. Then she appeared in the corner of the room. "See, I'd sneak into his room, stab him in his heart—if he ever had one—and then hang him out the castle window by his tiny dick."

Each man at the table covered their groin and moaned. Bryce, of course, laughed. Bea asked her when she'd gotten so vicious. She laughed and explained.

"The moment that they put that little girl in my arms and told me that she was mine. No one, not one person, is going not harm her without paying the consequences."

Again, they laughed, but Noah knew that she wasn't joking around. He would do the same, protect Lily with his life, but he had a feeling that Bryce would be a bit more vindictive about it, make the person suffer in ways that he never could. Yes, he thought, he was afraid of his mate. And with very good reason.

The dinner was nice, a loud friendly dinner. And when they were all ready to leave, he noticed that everyone put money on the table for a tip. He estimated that the waitress was going to leave with about four hundred dollars tonight. Smiling, he dropped another hundred on the table. Noah wanted to be able to come back here with a crowd, and not have no one want to wait on them. When they got out to the car, he stopped and just stared at the way each of the windows were covered up with bags. All but the windshield, thankfully.

"My goodness, you weren't kidding." He laughed with Bryce when she showed him what was in the back of her little car, as well as how much Kelly had been able to stuff into hers. "I take it we're going to have to go hunting for a crib tomorrow."

"No. William took care of that, he told me. As well as a dresser and rocker. Snow made the mobile that will hang from the bed, and there is a bassinet that will be delivered with all the things that we couldn't get in the vehicles."

They were getting used to carrying around a child. The car seat was still something that they had to play with to get in, and it wasn't until Devon showed them how to slip the seat on the base and hear it click that they got it. Sometimes, Noah thought, it took a visual to get it.

"I've been watching other people with their equipment. I don't think they actually call it that — something dirty, I was told, is what they call their equipment. Anyway, I've asked around, gotten the best ideas on stuff." Noah asked Devon where he could get the information that he had. "I'm telling you, Noah. You tell some woman that you're going to be a father soon, and they come out of the woodwork to give you a lesson on just about anything you want."

"Yes, but you must make sure that that's all they're giving you." Bryce laughed as Kelly continued, and Devon's face turned a very deep shade of red. "He was invited to this woman's house to see how the stroller worked to be put away. He told me he barely got out of there with his clothes still on. I've never seen him so shaken before. So, from then on, he took me with him on his hunts for information."

"Yeah, I found it to be safer. Not to mention, I got real information and not propositions." Devon hugged him and kissed Bryce on her cheek as the others loaded into their cars. "Come over tomorrow and we'll go over some of the things I think you can make an improvement on in your town. Things that we found out quite by accident. It might help you."

"Thanks." Noah started away when he turned back to his friend. "I have over forty eggs stashed away by my parents. Hatchlings of fallen dragons. I think, if we can, we should gather our forces. Perhaps bring in a few more like us to help out."

"I think you might be right. Are you and Bryce planning to raise all of them as your own?" He nodded. "Need any help with that? I mean, we're about to have our own; we could put another one with ours. I heard that it's best in raising dragons without real parents to have a mate, so to speak, to be with them."

"I think that's an excellent idea. But we really will need help. Just as your grandma said." Devon looked at the mountain, then back at him before Noah asked him if he was serious.

"I am. I'll talk to Kelly, but I don't think she's going to have any trouble being a mom to one. And maybe we can all learn from each other. I don't know any breeding pairs anymore. And even knowing ones from long ago, I wasn't into keeping up with what they were doing to keep them safe." Noah said that he'd not either. "All right. We'll add that to the talk. Also, if I were you, I'd not tell anyone but me about them. I'll tell Kelly and my grandma, but I'd wait on the others. I'm not saying that your parents will get them hurt, but it's been a very long time since dragons were born, and we don't want them to get overly excited if it doesn't work."

"I never thought of that."

Noah started for his car again and was inside and buckled

when he turned to look at his daughter. She was facing the back seat, as she should be, but they had a mirror now that showed her face.

She was sleeping peacefully, her little mouth puckered up like she was having a bottle. Bryce was in her car or they'd be riding together. Not that there was room in her car for the seat. Noah started the engine and started talking to his daughter.

"When you grow up, you're not to have a boyfriend unless I approve. You're not even going to date until you're about three hundred years old, all right?" He laughed at himself. "I love you, Lily girl. And I will forever. You just stick with us and we'll make sure that you'll be loved above everything else."

He was home when he realized again that he was a father. Being a dad, he thought, was better than sex. Noah glanced in the mirror, happy that Lily couldn't read minds. Laughing at his silliness, he took her out of the car and to the house. Life as he knew it was about to get very interesting.

Before You Go...

HELP AN AUTHOR

write a review

THANK YOU!

Share your voice and help guide other readers to these wonderful books. Even if it's only a line or two your reviews help readers discover the author's books so they can continue creating stories that you'll love. Login to your favorite retailer and leave a review. Thank you.

AWARD WINNING, BESTSELLING AUTHOR

Kathi Barton, winner of the Pinnacle Book Achievement award as well as a best-selling author on Amazon and All Romance books, lives in Nashport, Ohio with her husband Paul. When not creating new worlds and romance, Kathi and her husband enjoy camping and going to auctions. She can also be seen at county fairs with her husband who is an artist and potter.

Her muse, a cross between Jimmy Stewart and Hugh Jackman, brings her stories to life for her readers in a way that has them coming back time and again for more. Her favorite genre is paranormal romance with a great deal of spice. You can visit Kathi online and drop her an email if you'd like. She loves hearing from her fans. aaronskiss@gmail.com.

Follow Kathi on her blog: http://kathisbartonauthor. blogspot.com/